By John Fante

The Saga of Arturo Bandini:
   Wait Until Spring Bandini (1938, 1983)
   The Road to Los Angeles (1985)
   Ask the Dust (1939, 1980)
   Dreams from Bunker Hill (1982)

Dago Red (1940)
Full of Life (1952, 1988)
Brotherhood of the Grape (1977)
*The Wine of Youth: Selected Stories of
   John Fante* (1985)
1933 Was a Bad Year (1985)
West of Rome (1986)

JOHN FANTE

of **FULL**
LIFE

BLACK SPARROW PRESS

SANTA ROSA

1988

FULL OF LIFE. Copyright © 1952 by John Fante. Copyright © 1988 by Joyce Fante.

Library of Congress Cataloging-in-Publication Data

Fante, John, 1909-1983
    Full of life / John Fante.
    p.   cm.
    ISBN 0-87685-719-5 :   ISBN 0-87695-718-7 (pbk.) :
    ISBN 0-87685-720-9 (deluxe) :
    I. Title.
PS3511.A594F85   1988
813'.52 – dc19   87-27630
                                        CIP

This book is for

H. L. Mencken

with undiminished admiration.

FULL OF LIFE

ONE

It WAS a large house because we were people with big plans. The first was already there, a mound at her waist, a thing of lambent movement, slithering and squirming like a ball of serpents. In the quiet hours before midnight I lay with my ear to the place and heard the trickling as from a spring, the gurgles and sucks and splashings.

I said, "It certainly behaves like the male of the species."

"Not necessarily."

"No female kicks that much."

But she did not argue, my Joyce. She had the thing within her, and she was remote and disdainful and quite beatified.

Still, I didn't care for the bulge.

"It's unaesthetic," and I suggested she wear something to pack it in.

"And kill it?"

"They make special things. I saw them."

She looked at me with coldness — the ignorant one, the fool who had passed by in the night, a person no more, malefic, absurd.

The house had four bedrooms. It was a pretty house.

There was a picket fence around it. There was a tall peaked roof. There was a corridor of rose bushes from the street to the front door. There was a wide terra cotta arch over the front door. There was a solid brass knocker on the door. There was a 37 in the house number, and that was my lucky number. I used to cross the street and look at the whole thing with my mouth open.

My house! Four bedrooms. Space. Two of us lived there now, and one was coming. Eventually there would be seven. It was my dream. At thirty there was still time for a man to raise seven. Joyce was twenty-four. One every other year. One coming, six to go. How beautiful the world! How vast the sky! How rich the dreamer! Naturally we would have to add a room or two.

"Do you have whims? Peculiar tastes? I understand it happens. I been reading up on it."

"Of course not."

She was reading too: Gesell, Arnold: *Infant and Child in the Culture of Today.*

"How is it?"

"Very informative."

She looked through the French windows to the street. It was a busy street, just off Wilshire, where the busses roared, where the traffic sounded like the lowing of cattle, a steady roar sometimes zippered down the middle by the shriek of sirens, yet detached, far away, two hundred feet away.

"Can't we have some new drapes? Do we have to have yellow drapes and green valances?"

"Valance? What's a valance, Mother?"

"For God's sake don't call me that."

"Sorry."

She went back to Gesell, Arnold: *Infant and Child*

in the Culture of Today. There was solid reading comfort in pregnancy. The mound made a superb place to prop books, almost chin high, easy to turn pages. She was very pretty, with gray eyes incredibly bright. Something new was added to those eyes. Fearlessness. It was startling. You looked away. I glanced at the windows and found out what valances were because that was the only green at the windows, the skirt on top, ruffled.

"What kind of valance do you want, honey?"

"And please don't honey me. I don't like it."

I left her sitting there, the gray eyes bright with menace, the tight mouth around a cigarette holder, the long white fingers clutching Gesell. I walked out into my front yard and stood among roses and gloated over my house. The rewards of authorship. Me, author, John Fante, composer of three books. First book sold 2300 copies. Second book sold 4800 copies. Third book sold 2100 copies. But they don't ask for royalty statements in the picture business. If you have what they want at the moment they pay you, and pay you well. At that moment I had what they wanted, and every Thursday there came this big check.

A gentleman arrived about the valances. He was queer, with pellucid fingernails and a Paisley scarf under his belted sports coat. He wrung his tapered fingers and there was an intimacy between him and Joyce I could not share. They laughed and chatted over tea and cakes and she was delighted to have the companionship of a cock without spurs. He shuddered at the green valances, squealed in triumph as he tore them down and replaced them with blue. He sent for a truck, and the furniture was hauled away to be re-covered to match the valances.

Blue soothed Joyce. Now she was very happy. She

11

began to wash windows. She waxed floors. She didn't like the washing machine and did the laundry by hand. Twice a week we had someone in to do the heavy work, but Joyce fired the woman.

"I'll do it alone. I don't need help."

She got very tired from so much work. There were ten shirts piled up, carefully ironed. There was a red place on her thumb, a burn. Her hair hung down, she was haggard and indeed very tired. But the bump was firm, right out there, not tired at all.

"I can't go on much longer," she groaned. "This big house and all."

"But why do you do it? You know you mustn't."

"Do you like living in dirty surroundings?"

"Call somebody. We can afford it now."

Ah, she detested me, gritting her teeth, bravely pushing back her fallen hair. She picked up a dustcloth and staggered into the dining room, there to polish the table, taking long desperate strokes, utterly weary, propped on her elbows, gasping for breath.

"Let me help you."

"Don't touch me. Don't you dare!"

She sank into a chair, her hair hanging down, her burnt thumb aching, yet a badge for nobility, her bright weary eyes staring dangerously, the dust rag loose in her hand, a wistful smile on her lips, an expression denoting nostalgia, informing me that her thought was of a happier time, probably San Francisco in the summer of 1940, when her body was slender, when there were no back-breaking chores, when she was free and unmarried, climbing all over Telegraph Hill with her easel and paints, writing tragic love sonnets as she gazed at the Golden Gate.

"You ought to have a maid, all day long."

For those were the fat carnal days for the scribbler, and money was piling up with Thursday coming once a week, bringing my agent full of wit and camaraderie and what was left after he and the government cut up the Paramount check. And yet, there was plenty for us all.

"Go shopping, dear. Buy yourself some things."

God help me. I had forgotten the bulge, and I tried vainly to suck the words back into my mouth. But she did not forget and I had to pretend I wasn't looking when she came sweeping down the stairs, a white balloon of a wife, holding back belches and pacing here and there like a prisoner.

She said, "Stop staring."

She said, "I suppose you spend the whole day looking at slender actresses."

She said, "What are you thinking about?"

She said, "Never again. This is the first and last."

And sometimes I would look up to find her staring at me and shaking her head.

"In God's name, why did I ever marry you?"

I kept quiet, smiling foolishly, because I didn't know why either, but I was very glad and proud that she had.

§ § §

She got over the housework craze and the housekeeper was hired again. Now she became interested in gardening. She bought books and equipment. One day I came home to find ten sacks of steer manure in the garage. She pulled out the corridor of roses, twelve bushes, six on either side of the walk; she took a spade to them, gouged them out of the soil and dragged them into the back yard. She hacked out the roots with a hatchet. She put on gloves and spent the days crawling under hedges, putting in bulbs, smothering them with manure and peat moss, her knees showing dark red spots, her arms scratched. She developed a passion for keeping the grounds clean. Every day she made inspections, even in the alley, going about with a gunny sack, gathering up scraps of things. She took to burning everything around the place that wasn't nailed down — hedge clippings, leaves, pieces of wood. She dug a hole in the back yard for compost, storing lawn clippings in it, mixing manure with the clippings, watering it down, stirring it up now and then with a pronged tool.

I used to find her out there in the late afternoons when I drove into the garage. She would be standing at the incinerator, a forlorn figure with a white scarf around her head, dropping things into the fire, pieces of paper cartons stacked up, ready for burning, and Joyce staring at the flames, sometimes stirring the fire with a stick. She attained a frenzy for neatness and order around the incinerator, carefully fitting empty tin cans into each other, special boxes for the cans, special boxes for empty bottles. She made neat packages out of the day's garbage, wrapping it in newspapers and tying it with string.

In the night I heard her wandering around the house, banging the refrigerator door, flushing the toilet, turning on the radio downstairs, walking around in the back yard. From the window I saw her moving about in the moonlight, a bulging apparition in terry cloth, the round bump moving ahead of her with majestic aplomb, a book usually under her arm, usually Gesell, Arnold: *Infant and Child in the Culture of Today.*

14

"You can't sleep with me any more," she said. "Not ever."

"Not even after he's born?"

"It's a girl."

"Why do you keep insisting it's a girl?"

"I don't like boys. They're nasty. They cause all the trouble in the world."

"Girls cause trouble too."

"Not that kind of trouble."

"You'll love our son."

"Her name is Victoria."

"His name is Nick."

"I like Victoria better."

"You mean, Victor?"

"I mean, Victoria."

§ § §

There was also this passionate need for her. I had it from the first time I saw her. She went away that first time, she walked out of her aunt's house where we had met at tea, and I was no good without her, absolutely a cripple until I saw her again. But for her I might have lived out my life in other streams — a reporter, a bricklayer — whatever was at hand. My prose, such as it was, derived from her. For I was always quitting the craft, hating it, despairing, crumpling paper and throwing it across the room. But she could forage through the discarded stuff and come up with things, and I never really knew when I was good, I thought every line I ever wrote was no better than ordinary, for I had no way of being sure. But she could take the pages and find the good stuff and save it, and plead for more, so that it became habitual with me, and I wrote as best I could and handed her the pages, and she did a scissors-and-paste job, and when it was done, with a beginning and middle and end, I was more startled than seeing it in print, because at first I couldn't have done it alone.

Three years of this, four, five, and I began to have some notions about the craft, but they were her notions, and I never gave much thought to the others who might read my stuff, I only wrote it for her, and if she had not been there I might not have written it at all.

She didn't care to read me while she was pregnant. I brought her sequences from the script and she was not interested. That winter in her fifth month I wrote a short story and she spilled coffee on it — an unheard-of thing, and she read it with yawning attention. Before the baby she would have taken the manuscript to bed with her and spent hours pruning and fixing and making marginal notes.

Like a stone, the child got between us. I worried and wondered if it would ever be the same again. I longed for the old days when I could walk into her room and snatch up some intimacy of hers, a scarf or a dress or a bit of white ribbon, and the very touch had me reeling around, croaking like a bullfrog for the joys of my beloved. The chair she sat upon before the dressing table, the glass that mirrored her lovely face, the pillow upon which she laid her head, a pair of stockings flung to launder, the disarming cunning of her silk pants, her nightgowns, her soap, her wet towels still warm after her bath: I had need for these things; they were a part of my life with her, and the smear of lipstick made no difference, for the red had come from the warm lips of my woman.

Things were changed around there now. Her gowns were specially contrived, with a big hole in front through which leered the bump, her slips were impossible sacks, her flat shoes were strictly for the rice fields, and her blouses were like pup tents. What man could take such a gown and crush it to his face and shudder with the old familiar passion? Everything smelled different too. She used to use some magic called Fernery at Twilight. It was like breathing Chopin and Edna Millay, and when its fragrance rose from her hair and shoulders I knew the flag was up and that she had chosen to be pursued. She didn't use Fernery at Twilight any more: something else was substituted, a kind of Gayelord Hauser cologne, reeking of just plain good health, clean alcohol and simple soap. There was also the odor of vitamin tablets, of brewers' yeast and blackstrap molasses, and a pale salve to soothe her bursting nipples.

Lying in bed, I used to hear her slushing around, and wonder what was happening to us. I smoked in the darkness and moaned in the belief that she was driving me into another woman's arms. No, she didn't want me any more, she was forcing me to another woman, a mistress. But what mistress? For years I had been retired from the jungle where bachelors prowled. Where was I to find another woman, even if I wanted one? I saw myself skulking about on Santa Monica Boulevard, drooling at free women in dark, offbeat saloons, sweating out clever dialogue, drinking heavily to hide the stark ugliness of such romances. No, I could not be unfaithful to Joyce. I didn't even want to be unfaithful, and this worried me too. For was it not something of a custom for men to be unfaithful to their wives during confinement? It happened all the time out at the golf club: I heard it from all the guys. Then what was wrong with me?

Why wasn't I on the town, chafing for forbidden joys? And so I lay there, trying to coax up a flicker of that flame for strange fruit. But there was none.

§ § §

Still, I was glad to sleep alone. I had forgotten its pleasures. Four years we had lain side by side every night. I had become indoctrinated, accepting kicks without complaint, sleeping half-covered for over thirteen hundred nights. Of late her condition had rendered her worse. All sense of fair play had vanished. She had gone back to the primitive jungle where one fought for existence. Now she banged me with cold deliberation. At any hour of the night I found myself awakened by the snatch of a pillow from under my head, or the crunch of apples, or the refined torture of graham cracker crumbs against my side. She ate like a liberated refugee, coming to bed with big sandwiches and a pitcher of milk. Her milk consumption was staggering. She sat propped on pillows — mine and hers — eating and reading, mostly Gesell, Arnold: *Infant and Child in the Culture of Today*. Gesell, Arnold: *The Feeding Behavior of Infants: A Pediatric Approach to the Hygiene of Early Life* (with Ilg). Or Gilbert, Margaret: *Biography of the Unborn*.

Ten times a night she bolted from bed and dashed to the bathroom, flushing the toilet with defiant loudness, gargling, brushing her teeth, taking showers. Then back to bed with a hop, skip and jump, to enthrone herself in a place that had become an eating tavern, a bloated goddess comforted with pillows. If I moved or murmured, she cared not.

Aye, I was very glad to sleep alone, to lie in a bed

that was not also a delicatessen, to spread my arms and legs. It was an eerie pleasure, an atavistic revel, a return to Mother Earth. But she sensed my joy; she must have felt it through the wall, for she began to want things. A glass of milk, a sandwich, a match, a book. And if none of these, the light at my bedside would go on suddenly as she stood there, heavy and white and sad, saying quietly, "I can't sleep." It was a bed for one, and when she got in beside me there was no room at all unless she lay on her back with the mound sticking straight up. I backed away. It was like sleeping at the edge of a ditch.

"You hate me, don't you?" she said.

"I don't hate you."

"Why do you recoil? Is something wrong?"

"I can't sleep on top of you."

"You can, if you want."

"It leaves me cold. I'm sorry."

"Is it my breath?"

She blew it into my face. Her mouth that used to be warm and sweet now had that I'm-pregnant odor, not unpleasant but not pleasant either.

"It's on the fuzzy side."

For a little while she lay motionless, staring at the ceiling, the white mound moving up and down evenly, her hands folded across it. She began to cry, a little brook of tears coursing down her face.

"Honey! What is it!"

"I'm constipated," she sobbed. "I'm always consti-pated."

I held her close, smoothed back her hair, and kissed her warm forehead.

"Nobody loves a pregnant woman," she sobbed. "I

see it everywhere I go. On the street, in the stores, everywhere. They just stare and stare. It's awful."

"It's your imagination."

"That nice butcher. He used to be so sweet. Now he hardly even looks at me."

"Is that important?"

"It's *very* important!"

She wept a great deal that night, until her cheeks were puffed and there was no more tension, until the activity in the nest distracted her. She flung back the covers.

"Look."

The child squirmed like a kitten trapped in a balloon. It kicked painfully and you saw what looked like a tiny foot thumping away at the walls of its prison.

"Girls don't kick like that."

"Oh yes they do."

I put my ear against the soft warm mound and listened. It was the noise of a brewery, hissing pipes, fermenting vats, steaming bottle washers, and far away, on the roof of the brewery, someone calling for help. She took my hand.

"Feel the head."

I found the place; it was the size of a baseball. I felt what I thought were the hands, the feet. Then I got a start, but I said nothing lest I alarm her. There were two baseballs down there, there were *two* heads!

I told her it was wonderful, but my throat ached with fear because they were there all right: my adorable Joyce was carrying a most awful burden. I felt the place once more. There could be no doubt about it. The child was a monster. I gritted my teeth and lay back with a heart full of sickness, too frightened to speak. It was not brave to weep at a time like this, but I couldn't hold back my grief, and when she saw my tears she drenched me with tenderness, pleased with my weeping.

"You darling! You're so emotional."

I got hold of myself finally, but I wanted to be alone, to think things out, to call Dr. Stanley, to see if something couldn't be done. Her hunger gave me an excuse. She wanted an avocado sandwich. I rose to get it. But I had to be reassured that I had been wrong, and I came back.

"Let me feel it once more," I said.

"Of course."

My palm went over the place. I nearly fainted as the two protrusions pressed my hand. So it was true: we had begot a monster. I staggered downstairs. In the little room off the kitchen where we kept the telephone, in that small place I stood in the darkness, my head against the wall, and began to cry again.

Many things were clear now, the past revealed like an upturned garbage can. For it was not the fault of Joyce. Her life had been pure, spotless. But the premarital years of John Fante were foolish years of helter-skelter romances. There was much to bring blushes; there had been sins, grievous sins, and somewhere in this evil swirl the penalty had been sown, and now it was time to reap the wicked harvest.

I prepared the sandwich and brought it upstairs. Joyce was ready, floating in pillows, her arms out to receive the food. I couldn't bear it. I went downstairs, pulled the telephone into the kitchen, closed the doors, and dialed Dr. Stanley's number. He was at the hospital, waiting a delivery.

"I've got to see you right away."

"How's Joyce?"

"She's fine. It's me. And the baby."

"You?"

"I'll come down. It's very important."

I went upstairs again. Joyce had finished the sandwich. She lay full length, watching the mound.

"It's beautiful," she said. "Everything's beautiful."

She was soon asleep. I dressed and tiptoed
downstairs and out the side door to the garage. It was a
quarter to three, the streets deserted, a kind of madness in
the weird quiet of that vast metropolis. In ten minutes I
pulled up before St. James's Hospital. The receptionist told
me that Dr. Stanley was on the twelfth floor. He delivered
so many babies that the hospital reserved a room for him
in the maternity ward, where he could take cat naps. The
door to his room was open. He lay on a studio couch in
his shirt sleeves. My soft knock wakened him instantly and
he got to his feet. He was a small man with the face of a
baby, the large eyes expressing constant amazement. We
shook hands.

"You pregnant too?"

I told him it was no joking matter.

"Really?"

"I think I'm a very sick man."

"You look all right to me."

"Wait'll I tell you. It won't be so funny."

"I'm waiting. Sit down."

I dropped to his studio couch and fumbled for a
smoke. "There's something terribly wrong with the baby."

"I thought you said it was you."

"I'm coming to that. My sickness is related to the
baby. My disease."

"What disease is that?"

I couldn't tell him. I didn't want to tell him.

He said, "When did you have your last Wassermann?"

I told him about a year ago.

"But they're not infallible, Doc. I read it in a magazine article."

"Have you been unfaithful to your wife?"

"Yes. I mean, no. What I mean is, before I was married, there was a girl. I mean *some* girls. What I mean is, I'm worried, Doc."

"What makes you think there's something wrong with the baby?"

"I felt him."

"Felt him? How?"

"I put my hand on Joyce's stomach."

"And?"

"I felt something funny."

"What did it feel like?"

"I read that article in a medical journal, Doc. Sometimes the Wassermann is inaccurate."

"What did it feel like?"

Suddenly I didn't want to talk about it any more. Suddenly I realized I had been a fool, that the baby was fine, that it didn't have two heads, that the whole thing had come to my mind in one big undigested hunk of guilt-feeling, and that my being there on the twelfth floor of St. James's Hospital at three-thirty in the morning talking to Dr. Stanley in the maternity ward was absolutely ridiculous. I wanted to be out of there, in my car, on my way home, to crawl into bed and cover my head with blankets and wake up bright and fresh to a new day. Instead, I stood before this tired doctor, pestering him with my idiocies, and there was nothing to do but make some kind of civilized exit.

"Dr. Stanley, I think I've made a grave mistake."

"So you felt the baby, and it felt funny. Tell me about this funny feeling. Describe it."

The answer was: two heads. Better to leap from the window than say it.

"I'm sorry, Doc. I was wrong. I just thought I felt something. I'm sorry I bothered you."

I began to leave, backing out, but he stopped me and pushed a buzzer in the wall, and in a moment a nurse was there. He ordered me to take off my jacket and roll up my sleeve, because he wanted to reassure me, to rid my mind of any doubts.

"But it's preposterous, Doc. There's nothing wrong with my blood—absolutely nothing."

He wound a rubber hose around my arm until the veins bulged and I felt the prick of the needle and watched my own blood being sucked into a syringe.

"Come back tomorrow night," he said. "Any time. I'll be here with your analysis."

I rolled down my sleeve and put on my coat.

"This is silly, Doc. There's nothing wrong with me."

"Go home. Get some sleep."

Through the quiet streets I drove home, thinking of those other girls, sweet Avis and dear Monica, and I was suddenly very lonely for them after all those years, for they had been so beautiful and so tender, with such superb bodies, not bloated by pregnancy, girls I longed for with a ravishing cloying desire now, gone forever, and I almost cried as I realized I could never have them again. This was marriage, this entombment, this vile prison where a man out of an overpowering desire to be good and decent and wholesome allows himself to be made a fool of at three in the morning, with no reward save children, and a thankless brood at that. I could see them now, my children, kicking me into the street in my old age, running me out of the house, signing papers so they could get me an old-age pension and wash their hands of me, a doddering old man who had given the best years of his life in honest toil that they might enjoy the full taste of life. Here was my thanks!

§ § §

The next night I was back at the hospital, waiting for Dr. Stanley's report on my blood analysis. I hated being there. Dr. Stanley was delivering a baby, and the nurse asked me to wait in the Fathers' Room. Two other fathers were there, one asleep in a leather chair, the other reading a magazine. I smoked cigarettes and paced up and down. It was preposterous. I didn't belong there—yet. But there I was, going through all the motions, and the man with the magazine thought we shared a common fate.

"How's your missus?" he asked.

"Fine. How's yours?"

"Not good."

His eyes were slits of red, his face beaten with worry. His hair was long and he needed a shave. "She's been in labor thirteen hours."

"Sorry to hear it."

"They may do a Caesarean."

This was no place for me. I was profaning this place where life was born, where women suffered and men worried. These people had real problems, but I was only fooling around, a victim of myself. Then the nurse appeared.

"Mr. Fante . . ."

The Caesarean father shook my hand. The other man got up too and offered his hand. They wished me good luck. I thanked them and went down the hall after the nurse to Dr. Stanley's little room. He was there, holding a slip of paper.

"There's nothing wrong with you."

"I knew it all the time."

He smiled.

"What'd you have for dinner last night?"

I told him: spaghetti, meat balls, salad, wine, ice cream. "Why, Doc?"

"Cholesterol. The analysis shows an excess. What you had for dinner explains it."

"Cholesterol! Good God, Doc! I read about cholesterol in a magazine. It's dangerous. It blocks up the arteries and causes heart attacks. I read about it in *Hygeia*."

"Do you have heart trouble?"

"Not yet, but . . ."

"Forget it."

"Cholesterol! Me, of all people."

He advised me to stop reading medical articles and forget the whole matter, but I could not forget it, staggering down the hall, groping for the elevator button, sweat popping from my palms, going down the elevator shaft, bubbles in my belly, cholesterol, heart attacks, author collapses and dies of sudden attack, down into the street, staggering to my car, sitting behind the wheel, feeling my pulse, counting it against my wrist watch, John Fante, taken suddenly, career cut short, seventy-two beats a minute, my God, cholesterol: I had to look it up, do some more research, get better acquainted with this dread substance.

Joyce was asleep when I got home. It was around midnight. I went to bed with the light on, making frequent pulse counts. It was a rough night. I remember the coming of daylight, and then I was asleep. At noon I woke feeling fine.

Joyce was in her room writing letters.

"How'd you sleep?"

"Terrible," she said. "I was awake all night."

"Let's not have spaghetti any more. It's full of cholesterol."

"Is it, really?"

"Let's have green salads, carrots. Fresh vegetables right out of the soil, crisp and good for you."

I went into the bathroom and took my pulse. It was sixty-eight. Down four. A slow pulse was better than a fast pulse. That was certain. I had read it in several periodicals.

§ § §

At 9:27 on the morning of March 18th, in the seventh month of her confinement, Joyce Fante fell through the kitchen floor of our house. The sheer weight of her—she had gained twenty-five pound and tipped the scale at one hundred and forty-four—plus the condition of the woodwork, came to a shuddering climax as the termite-infested floor boards collapsed beneath the tearing linoleum and the woman with the big bump sank to the ground three feet below.

I was upstairs in the bathtub at the time, and I remember distinctly the minute events coming before and after the calamity. First there was this fine quiet morning, all decked out in the golden gloss of the sun, there was the placidity of the bath, the mysterious evocations of confined water, the conjuring of faraway things, and then, from somewhere, from everywhere, the quivering of the atmosphere, the ominous portent of chain reaction in fissionable materials. A moment later I heard her scream. It was a theater scream, Barbara Stanwyck trapped by a rapist, and it plucked my spinal column like a giant's fingers.

I jumped out of the tub and opened the door. Down there I could hear Joyce shrieking. My one thought was the child—the precious white melon.

"I'm coming, Joyce. Be brave, darling. I'm coming!"

I had a gun in my room, but in that moment my only thought was her need for me. Even as I dashed downstairs naked and frightened I somehow knew those were my last mortal steps, that we would die together, that we might have lived had I been armed.

At first I didn't see her. Then I found her before the kitchen range, even as she had fallen, snug in the neat cave-in, but cut off as if she were a midget, a slice of ham in one hand, a skillet in the other, with many eggs broken and leaking around her. She was more angry than hurt, melted butter trickling from her hair and mingling with her tears, stringy egg yolk dripping from her elbows.

"Get me out of here, if you please."

I pulled her out. She was surprisingly calm. I stood looking down at the floor.

"Woh hoppen?"

Her fingers probed the mound, searching for life. She went to the telephone and began dialing. "Tell Dr. Stanley to hurry. It's an emergency." She hung up and walked to the stairs.

"How'd it happen?"

She didn't answer. A moment later she was in bed. I buzzed around, trying to get her things. She was white-faced but very calm. Then she closed her eyes. It scared me. I shook her.

"You all right?"

"I think so."

She closed her eyes again. I got scared again. I ran downstairs and got her some brandy. She didn't want any. I asked her not to close her eyes.

"I'm just resting."

"I don't think you ought to close your eyes."

"I'm only resting until the doctor comes."

Dr. Stanley was there in twenty minutes. I took him upstairs and he began to examine her. The fall had caused no injury to herself or the child. He put away his stethoscope. I went downstairs to the front door with him. I thought we should have a man-to-man talk about all this.

"Anything I can do, Doc?"

"No. Not a thing."

There was cold glitter in his eyes. He was getting tired of us. We were taking up a lot of his time.

I went back to the kitchen and stood before the hole in the floor. Fungus and termites had eaten the wood. It crumbled like soft bread in my hands. I crossed the room to the sink and banged my heel against the floor. The blow punctured it, leaving a hole. Apparently the entire floor was rotted. In the breakfast nook I hit the wall with my fist. My knuckles sank through spongy plaster and wood. I climbed the table in the breakfast nook to check the ceiling, but my weight made the table legs sink into the floor. I walked into the dining room and stood before an expanse of a pale green wall, freshly painted, immaculate. I raised my fist to let fly, but inside me there was a great sickness and I was afraid to strike.

My house! Why had this happened to John Fante? What had I done to upset the rhythm of the stars in their courses? I went back to Joyce's hole and stared. I picked up a piece of rotten wood. There I saw them, the little white beasties, crawling in the dead wood, the wood of my house, and I took one between my fingers, his little white legs pawing the air — a termite, an inhuman beast, and I killed it; I, who couldn't bear killing anything, but I had to snuff out his life for what he and his vile breed had done to my house. It was the first termite I had ever killed. All those years I had seen them about, watching them in curious admiration. I was a firm believer in the live-and-let-live philosophy, and this was my thanks, this loathsome treachery. Well, there was something wrong with my thinking, there had to be some change in my relations with insects, the hard reality of the facts had to be reckoned, and I started then and there to kill them, breaking the wood open, squashing them, crushing out their nefarious little lives as they ran panic-stricken through my fingers.

§ § §

A realtor named J. W. Randall had sold us the house. He was lean and sharp, a cowboy retired from the saddle. He came to the house and inspected the damage. He crushed the pulpy wood between his fingers, brushing away the termites swarming over the long hairs on the back of his hand.

"Mr. Randall, we've been cheated. I'm going to sue."

"Can't sue me."

"You arranged the sale."

"Smith's your man. Sue Smith."

Smith was the termite inspector.

"You hear that, Joyce? Smith's our man. We'll drag him through the courts."

Joyce said, "Mr. Randall, you're a scoundrel."

He straightened.

"Now just a minute, young woman."

She walked away from him. Mr. Randall was injured and angry. He stalked out of the house. I chased after him. He got into his car, surly and breathing heavily through his nose.

"I been in this business thirty years. Hell-fire, man! I *made* Wilshire Boulevard! And she calls me a scoundrel."

"She's upset, Mr. Randall. It's her condition."

"Son, let me give you a bit of advice. I'm a grand-father. Got four grandchildren. Better calm that young lady down. Pregnant woman's got to have pure thoughts. No wonder we got so much juvenile delinquency. Watch it, boy. I know what I'm talking about."

"What about Smith?"

"Sue the man."

Smith could not be found. I went to the garage that had been his place of business, a stucco shack behind a carpenter shop on Temple Street. He called his company Murder, Inc. He was gone. Nobody knew anything about him, except that he was fond of angelica. I talked to a lawyer. He told me it would be two years before we could get a court date, and without Smith we had no case. A con-tractor came to the house and gave us an estimate for repairs. He said four thousand.

Joyce: "We could have ten babies with that."

Four thousand! It was a knife through my heart. I

staggered into the kitchen, sick and wounded. The main damage was there in the kitchen. On hands and knees under the sink I groped, poking around. There was a noise. I put my ear to the floor. Down there, only inches away, I could hear them, the vile beasts, actually gnawing my wood. It was the rhythmic grinding of thousands of tiny jaws, feeding on the flesh and blood of John Fante.

Then, suddenly, I knew what to do. Like cool waters, the thought bathed me. Like parting clouds, the storm had passed and he was there, bold as sunlight, the greatest bricklayer in all California, the noblest builder of them all! Papa! My own flesh and blood, old Nick Fante. I ran to the stairs and called Joyce.

"How blind we are! How stupid!"

"Why?"

"My father!"

"Wonderful!"

She hurried downstairs and we grabbed one another. She loved Papa too, and he adored her.

"He'll do it for nothing. We'll save thousands."

But she grew wistful, serious.

"Promise me something."

"Certainly."

"That you'll never treat our child the way your father treated you."

"He was a good father, rough but good."

"Once he beat your bare flesh with a trowel. Your sister Stella told me."

"I had it coming. I sold his concrete mixer and bought a bicycle."

"You don't beat children any more. It's been disproved. You deny them some privilege."

"He denied me the bicycle. Besides, it was the only concrete mixer he had."

"Have you read *Wolf Child and Human Child*, by Gesell?"

I hadn't.

"Every father should read it. It's basic."

"I'll read it on my way up North."

TWO

MY MAMA AND PAPA lived in San Juan, in the Sacramento Valley, a dozen miles down the road from the state capitol. They were in halcyon retirement now, drawing state pensions, floating through the most placid passage of their lives. They lived in a four-room redwood cottage, with a capacious fig tree shading the back yard. A dozen hens clucked in the chicken yard, loft fowl, glutted by fallen figs and luscious Tokays from vines menacing the back fence. These hens debouched massive eggs whose warmth Mama loved against her palms in ironic nostalgia, for there was once a time in the life of this mother when children outnumbered the eggs.

On a barrel under the fig tree slept Papa's four cats, glistening Egyptian deities, sleek from beef hearts, calves' brains and milk. These four cats had replaced four children who had grown up to leave the Valley and marry and acquire enfeebled eyes and partial dentures because in that earlier time work was scarce and Papa never earned enough to feed his children regularly on beef hearts, calves' brains and milk.

They lived in serene loneliness, my Papa and Mama, reading the *Sacramento Bee* and listening to the radio, gathering eggs and raking the big green fig leaves, two people in their late sixties, eager for the postman who no longer terrified them with bills and too seldom arrived with letters from the children who were gone.

It wasn't necessary for Stella to write. She and her husband lived on a farm outside San Juan and came twice a week with baskets of zucchini, tomatoes, peaches, oranges and butter.

Stella brought her little girls, and on hot afternoons Papa sat with them under the fig tree, sneaking them sips of iced wine, telling them stories, and wondering why in the name of Our Lady of Mount Carmel he had no grandsons. For Papa was sixty-seven, and though he admired the non-Italian girls his sons had married, he also suspected them of trickery in the matter of procreation, of not knowing how to work at it.

Once a week Joe Muto came down the road in his Ford truck to deliver two gallons of claret at fifty cents a gallon. He liked bringing his four grandsons, little boys with black eyes and Muto faces, and Papa scowled at them because they were not his.

Life without grandsons was not life at all. Sitting under the fig tree, Papa tilted the claret jug from his shoulder, lapped the cool wine and brooded. In the late afternoon the mailman drove by, and Mama would be at the gate near the box, waiting, pretending to pull weeds here and there. If there was no mail, she pulled another weed or two, peered nervously down the road toward Sacramento, and came back to the house, wincing on arthritic feet. Day after day Papa watched this happen. Finally his patience would break.

"Bring pen and ink!"

Dutifully Mama would come from the house with

a tablet and writing materials, set them on the barrel under the fig tree, and settle herself to take another letter from Papa to her three sons: one in Seattle, another in Susanville, and the third in the South. They were letters she never sent, a gesture of appeasement, because Papa derived much satisfaction from the dictation, it soothed his nerves as he paced back and forth through the hissing leaves, now and then stopping to take thoughtful gulps of claret.

"Send it to all of them. Write it plain. Put it down just like I tell you. Don't change a word."

She would dip the pen, her knees against the barrel, as she sat uncomfortably on an apple box.

Dear Sons:
Your mother is fine. I'm fine too. We don't need you boys any more. So have a good time, laugh and play, and forget all about your father. But not your mother. Don't worry about your father. It's your mother. Your father worked hard to buy you shoes and put you through school. He don't regret nothing. He don't need anything. So have a good time, boys, laugh and play, but think about your mother some time. Write her a letter. Don't write to your father because he don't need it, but your mother's getting old now, boys. You know how they get when they get old. So have a good time while you're young. Laugh and play and think about your mother some time. Makes no difference about your father. He never did need your help. But your mother gets lonesome. Have a good time. Laugh and play.
Yours truly,
Nick Fante

And when Mama was finished, he would sip from the jug, smack his lips, and add: "Send it air mail."

§   §   §

I reached San Juan at noon, flying up from Burbank and taking the bus out of Sacramento. The folks lived at the edge of town, where the city pavement ended and the last street light was a hundred feet away. Walking down the road past the old board fence, I could see Papa under the fig tree. His drawing board was spread over the barrel; on it were pencils, rulers, a T square. The cats slept in the swing, piled in hot furry confusion.

Hearing the whine of the gate, Papa turned, his phlegmatic eyes squinting for range through waves of gossamer heat. It was my first visit in six months. Except for his vision, he was superb. He had thick bricky hands and a sun-baked neck, handsome as sewer pipe. I was within fifty feet of him before he recognized me. I dropped my overnight bag and put out my hand.

"Hello, Papa."

He had the hands of Beelzebub, horny and calloused, the gnarled oft-broken fingers of a bricklayer. He looked down at the grip.

"What you got in there?"

"Shirts and things."

He inspected me carefully.

"New suit?"

"Fairly new."

"How much?"

I told him.

"Too much."

Emotion was piling up inside him. He was very glad I had come home, but he tried not to show it, his chin trembling.

"Smell the peppers? Mama's frying peppers."

From the back porch it came, a river of ambrosial redolence, fresh green peppers sizzling in golden olive oil, charmed with the fragrance of garlic and the balm of rosemary, all of it mingled with the scent of magnolias and the deep green richness of vineyards in the back country.

"Smells good. How you feel, Papa?"

He was shrinking. Every year he receded a little, or so it seemed. Neither of us were tall men, but now in his late years he gave me the sense of being taller than he was. The yard was smaller too, and I was surprised at the fig tree. It was not nearly as big as I imagined.

"The baby. How's the little bambino?"

"Six weeks more or less."

"And Miss Joyce?" He worshipped her. He could not bring himself to call her simply by her name.

"She's fine."

"She carry him high?" He touched the chest. "Or low?" His hand dropped to his stomach.

"High. Way up, Papa."

"Good. Little boy, that means."

"I don't know."

"How you mean, don't know?"

"You can't be sure of these things."

"You can, if you do the right thing."

He frowned, looked straight into my eyes.

"You been eating plenty eggs, like I told you?"

"I don't like eggs, Papa."

He sighed and shook his head.

"Remember what I told you? Eat plenty eggs. Three, four, every day. Otherwise, it's a girl." He made a face as he added: "You want a girl?"

"I'd like a boy, Papa. But you have to take what you get."

It worried him. Back and forth he paced through the fig leaves. "That's no way to talk. That's no good."

"But Papa . . ."

He whirled around.

"Don't *but* me. Don't *Papa* me! I told you, and I told you, all of you: Jim, Tony, you. I said: eggs. Plenty eggs. Look at them. Jim: nothing. Married two years. Tony: nothing. Married three years. And you. What you got? Nothing." He moved close to me, his face near mine, his claret breath bursting at me. "Remember what I said about oysters? You got money now. You can afford oysters."

I remembered a post card dictated to Mama and sent to Joyce and me on our honeymoon at Lake Tahoe. The card said I should eat oysters twice a week to induce fertility and the conception of male children. But I had not followed the advice because I didn't like oysters. I had no personal animosity toward oysters. I simply didn't like their taste.

"I don't care for oysters, Papa."

It staggered him. With a limp neck and open jaws, he flung himself into the swing and wiped his forehead. The cats wakened, yawning with sharp pink tongues.

"Holy Mother of Heaven! So this is the end of the Fante line."

"I think it's a boy, Papa."

"You think!" He cursed me, a scathing coruscation of firecracker Italian. He spat at my feet, sneering at my gabardine and my sport moccasins. He took the stub of a Toscanelli cigar from his shirt and jammed it into his teeth. He lit up, flung the match away.

40

"You think! Who asked you to think? I *told* you: oysters. Eggs. I been through it. I give you advice from experience. What you been eating — candy, ice cream? Writer! Bah! You stink like the plague."

This was my Papa for sure. He had not shrunk, after all. And the fig tree was as big as ever.

"Go see your Mama." There was sarcasm in his voice. "Go tell her what a fine big boy she's got."

§   §   §

Greeting Mama was always the most difficult task of a homecoming. My Mama was the fainting type, specially if we had been away more than three months. Inside three months there was some control over the situation. Then she only teetered dangerously and appeared about to fall over, giving us time to catch her before the collapse. An absence of a month entailed no problem at all. She merely wept for a few moments before the usual barrage of questions.

But this was a six-month interval and experience had taught me not to burst in on her. The technique was to enter on tiptoe, put your arms around her from behind, quietly announce yourself, and wait for her knees to buckle. Otherwise she would gasp, "Oh, thank God!" and go plummeting to the floor like a stone. Once on the floor she had a trick of sagging in every joint like a mass of quicksilver, and it was impossible to lift her. After futile pawing and grunting on the part of the returned son she got to her feet by her own power and immediately started cooking big dinners. Mama loved fainting. She did it with great artistry. All she needed was a cue.

Mama loved dying, too. Once or twice a year, and

specially at Christmas time, the telegrams would come, announcing that Mama was dying again. But we could not risk the possibility that for once it was true. From all over the Far West we would rush to San Juan to be at her bedside. For a couple of hours she would die, making a clatter of saucers in her throat, showing only the whites of her eyes, calling us by name as she entered the valley of shadows. Suddenly she would feel much better, crawl out of her death bed, and cook up a huge ravioli dinner.

She was at the stove, her back to me, as I entered the kitchen and moved quietly toward her. Midway, she sensed my presence, turning slowly, a spatula in her hand. A kind of nausea seemed to grip her, a disembodiment, the elevator zooming down out of control, the dizzy moment before the plunge from a great height; her eyes rolled, the blood fled from her quick white face, the strength left her fingers and the spatula hit the floor.

"Johnny! Oh, thank God!"

I rushed forward and she fell into my arms, her hair the color of white clouds at my shoulder, her hands around my neck. But she did not lose consciousness. She seemed to be having a heart attack. I knew this from the quick rasping gasps, the quivering of her small frame. Carefully I led her to a chair at the kitchen table. She lay back, her mouth open, smiling bravely, her left arm helpless at her side, and you could see that she was trying to lift the arm and was without strength.

"Water. Water . . . please."

I brought her a glass and put it to her lips. She sipped wearily, too far gone, too drained, only seconds from the other shore.

"My arm . . . no feelings . . . my chest . . . pain . . .

my boy . . . the baby . . . I won't live to see . . ."

She collapsed face down on the checkered red and white oilcloth. I was reasonably sure she was all right, but when I gently turned her face and saw the gray purple of her cheeks I felt that I was wrong this time, and I yelled for Papa.

"Get a doctor! Hurry."

It restored her strength. Slowly she raised her head.

"I'm better. It was only a little attack."

It was my turn to weaken, relieved, suddenly exhausted. I threw myself into a chair and tried to unravel my fingers as I groped for a smoke. Papa entered.

"What's going on?"

My Mama smiled bravely. She was so pleased to see me distraught. She could not doubt my love now. She felt quite strong again.

"It's nothing. Nothing at all."

She was very happy. She purred. She rose and came around to where I sat and took my head in her arms and stroked my hair.

"He's tired from his trip. Get him a glass of wine."

We understood, Papa and I. There was a rumble of curses in his throat, scarcely audible, as he opened the icebox and removed a decanter of wine. He took a glass from the cupboard and filled it. Mama smiled, watching. He glanced at her angrily.

"You cut that out."

The great green eyes of my Mama opened their widest.

"Me?"

"You cut out that stuff."

I drank the wine. It was very fine wine, out of the

warm soil of those very plains, chilled delicately by ice. Mama was glad to have me in her kitchen. I could see her spine straighten, her shoulders rising. She took the glass from my hand and drained it. Then she looked at me carefully.

"Such a pretty shirt. I'll wash and iron it before you leave."

§ § §

We ate the peppers with goat's cheese, salted apples, bread and wine. Mama's tongue whirred incessantly, a trapped moth free at last. Normally Papa would have quieted her down, but the son was home and this was cause for relaxing the rules. In a little while her chatter would suddenly exasperate him, and she would slip back to her cocoon of respectful silence. We ate while Mama talked and walked around the kitchen, filling the room with thought fragments. An electric fan purred on the icebox, turning left and right and back again. It seemed to be following Mama around the room, like a face staring in blank astonishment.

Mama said:

The winter had been cold and wet. Stella's children were beautiful. There were moths in the clothes closet. She had dreamed of her dead sister Katie. The price of chicken feed was too high. My brother Jim ate dirt as a baby. Sometimes she had shooting pains in her legs. It was bad luck to wash diapers in the moonlight. When you lose something, pray to St. Anthony. The cats were killing blackbirds. Bacon should not be kept on ice. She was afraid of snakes. The roof leaked. There was a new postman. Her mother died of gangrene poisoning. Ice was bad for the stomach. Pregnant women shouldn't look at frogs or lizards. Love was more important than money. She was lonesome.

Her hands rested on my shoulders.

"If you would write just once a week . . ."

For half an hour she had talked constantly. It was a soothing drone we identified but ignored. Papa and I finished the peppers. He filled my glass.

Then Mama said, "You planted the seeds for your baby in this house. Right in this house. It was the eighth of August, last year, during that night."

It was her first statement that sank home. I stopped eating and looked at her. Then I remembered. Joyce and I had indeed been in San Juan last August. We had slept on the studio couch in Mama's parlor. I remembered the night very well. It was a squeaky studio couch and we decided not to try anything. There had been no conception that night. Mama was all wrong about that.

"No, she's not," Papa said.

"What makes you so sure?"

Mama smiled. "Because I sprinkled salt in your bed."

Papa grinned.

"That's right. Salt in the bed. I gave the order."

It was very annoying. They were quite smug, taking credit for everything. I told them I didn't remember salt in the bed. This amused Mama.

"Of course not. I put it under the sheets."

Papa chuckled.

"So now you're gonna have a baby."

"Salt," I said. "What poppycock!"

"Cock nothing," Papa said. "How do you suppose you was born?"

"The usual way."

"Wrong again. Salt in the bed. I put it there myself."

I pushed my glass forward, to be filled again.

"Superstition. Ignorance."

He refused to fill my glass.

"Don't call me ignorance. I'm your Papa."

"I didn't say you were ignorant."

"I want respect for your Papa. This is your Papa's house. Here, I'm the boss."

He was red-faced with quick indignation, filling the glass with trembling fingers, spilling some of the wine. It was bad luck to spill wine. You warded off the ill fortune by making the sign of the cross through the spilled liquor. This Mama did.

"Your Papa's right," she soothed. "We didn't have any garlic in the house that night, so Papa used salt. It was his own idea."

"Garlic?" I looked into Mama's large green eyes. "Why garlic?"

"To put in the keyhole."

"Is that suppose to bring babies?"

"Not plain babies — *boy* babies."

That stopped me cold. It brought a triumphant sneer from Papa.

"Look who's calling his Papa ignorance! He don't know nothing."

I swallowed wine, said nothing.

"The same with Tony and Jim," Mama said.

"Garlic in the keyhole when they were born?"

"Both times," Papa said.

"And Stella?"

But I already knew his answer:

"No garlic, no salt, no nothing."

He would argue, so I kept still. He filled my glass again.

"I only went to the third grade," he mused. "But you — you're supposed to have a big education, high school, two years of college, and you're still a kid. You got lots to learn."

I was not so ignorant as he imagined. I had learned plenty in that family, ever since childhood, all sorts of priceless learning handed down from generations of Abruzzian forebears. But I found much of this knowledge difficult to use. For example, I had known for years that the way to avoid witches was to wear a fringed shawl, for the attacking witch got distracted counting the fringes and never bothered you. I also knew that cow's urine was simply marvelous for growing hair on bald heads, but up to now I had no occasion to apply this information. I knew, of course, that the cure for measles was a red scarf, and the cure for sore throat was a black scarf. As a child, whenever I got a fever, my Grandma always fastened a piece of lemon to my wrist; it lowered the fever every time. I knew too that the evil eye caused headaches, and my Grandma used to send me out in the rain to plunge a knife in the ground, thus diverting the lightning from our house. I knew that if you slept with the windows open, all the witches in the community entered your house, and that if you *must* sleep in the fresh air, a bit of black pepper sprinkled along the window sill caused the witches to sneeze and back off. I also knew that the way to avoid infection when visiting a sick friend was to spit on his door. All these things, and many more, I had known for years, and never forgotten. But you live and learn, and the garlic-and-salt treatment for the marriage bed was something else again. My Papa was probably right: I wasn't so smart, after all. Still I had strong doubts about Joyce's pregnancy beginning that night last November on Mama's studio couch.

§ § §

Lunch was over. Papa pushed back his chair.

"Get your hat."

I never wore a hat. He meant that I should follow him. We went down the porch steps to the street. He poked inside the mailbox, drew out a dry cigar butt, and lit up. The smoke hung so motionless in the quiet air that he had to brush it with his hand. Heat filled the mighty sky, blue and vast and endless. To the east the Sierra Nevadas raised proud heads, the snows of last winter still upon them.

The street before the house was deserted. Ten years ago San Juan had been a hustling town with packing sheds and importance as a grape center. The state highway used to run right through the business center, but the war came and the highway was rerouted, so that it skirted the town now, and the town was slowly dying. The highway was beyond the peach and hop fields now, and tourists swept past and never knew that beyond the orchards lay a community of six thousand.

"Where we going?"

Without answering he started up the street. We passed three small homes and then there were no more houses, only the broken asphalt with weeds forcing their way through the cracks, and vineyards on both sides of the road, fanning off to the north and south, thousands of acres of muscats and Tokays, a sea of green silence.

"Where we going?"

He walked a little faster, until we came to a place where the road turned and went downhill. This was Joe Muto's land. I recognized the white-topped markings of his fence posts. It was the edge of the Muto vineyard — uncultivated, shrouded in a disordered growth of scrub oak, manzanita, and the last of what had once been a lemon grove. Everything grew wild here, three or four acres which, for one reason or another, Joe Muto had not planted to grapes. My Papa stood before this mass of green confusion and swept it with a gesture of his cigar.

"There she is."

He went plowing through the weeds and I followed. In the very middle of the plot, on a promontory overlooking the whole area, he stopped to open out his arms.

"Here she is. What I'm dreaming about."

He bent down to pull up a clump of wild poppies. They came, roots and all, the black tenacious soil hugging the roots. He crushed the roots in his fist, and the warm wet soil was molded to the shape of his hand.

"Everything grows here. Plant a broomstick, she'll grow."

I saw the meaning of it all.

"You'd like to own this, Papa? You want to buy it?"

"Not for me." He grinned and kicked the ground. "It's for the baby. This is where he's gonna live. Right here." He kicked at the earth again. "It's what I'm dreaming about. You and Miss Joyce and the little boy. Me and Mama down the road. Big place. Four acres. For you. For your children."

"But Papa . . ."

"No buts. I'm your Papa. All that junk you write. You got money?"

"I got a few dollars, Papa."

"You got two thousand dollars?"

"Yes."

"Buy it. I talked to Joe Muto. He's my *paisano*. He won't sell to nobody but me."

What could I say to this man — my Papa? What could I say to this work-wracked face, hardened by the years, softened now by his dream, moving about with his feet on his dream? There was the blue sky and the old lemon trees, and the tall weeds purring like an old love at his legs; and they were there already, his grandchildren, breathing that air, tossing in the grass, their bones fed by this soil that was his dream.

What could I say to this man? Could I tell him that I had bought a house in that jumbled perversity called Los Angeles, right off Wilshire Boulevard, a plot of ground fifty by a hundred fifty, and teeming with termites? Had I told him, the earth would have swallowed me, the sky would have crushed me.

"Let me think about it, Papa. I'll see what I can do."

"Now I'll show you something else."

I followed him back to the road, wondering how I should break the news. . . . For he had to be told about the house in Los Angeles. He should have been told long ago. Yet there had been no deliberate concealment. I had simply forgotten to mention it, no more and no less.

We walked back to the house and I could feel his joy. He lit a brand-new fresh cigar and led me to the drawing board on the barrel under the fig tree. Here were the plans for the house he proposed to build on those acres.

They were beautiful plans. A stone house it was, the stones free for gathering from a field not far away. There were three fireplaces, one in the kitchen, one in the living

room, and one out of doors. It was a long L-shaped ran-
cho, a one-story house with a tile roof.

"Last a thousand years," he said. "These are twelve-
inch walls, full of steel tie rods."

"Fine, Papa."

"I'll build it for nothing. You help me. I got my pension. I don't want any more."

"Yes. Fine."

Yes, and yes, and yes. Until he had explained the
last stone and beam, until he was very happy, sucking his
cigar and drinking wine. Then the afternoon coolness drifted
through from the green vineyard seas and he was sated with
so much talking. He rolled up the drawings, put out his
cigar, laid the butt in the crotch of the fig tree, and stretched
out on the lawn swing. A great and wonderful peace shone
on his face. No happier man lived on this earth. He closed
his eyes and slept. Had he died at that moment, he would
have gone straight to paradise.

§ § §

One thing about your Mama: nothing you do alarms
her. If I had walked into the kitchen and told her that I had
just slit Papa's throat, she would have answered, "That's
too bad—where is he?"

I found her at the table, shelling peas. It is so easy
to talk to your Mama; even the things she doesn't understand, she makes herself understand. Sitting there, I laid
out the whole situation about the house in Los Angeles. No
recriminations; she did not sigh, nor cluck her tongue, nor
admonish me on what I should have done. She shelled peas
and listened quietly as I told her why I had come to San

Juan, and how, under the circumstances, I was afraid to tell Papa I already owned a house.

"I'll tell him. Don't you worry about it."

But I didn't want to be around when she told him. "I'll take a walk downtown."

"Don't you worry."

I rose to leave. She stopped me. Something bothered her.

"You and Joyce. Do you sleep American style?" She meant, did we sleep separately?

"Now that she's pregnant, we sleep American."

"What a shame. The baby won't know you."

"We'll get acquainted after he's born."

"Sleep Italian style. You don't understand about babies. It's lonely down in the womb. He's there, all by himself. He needs his father."

I didn't want to discuss the matter with my mother. "I'll be back at seven. You tell Papa everything as soon as he wakes up."

It was five blocks to downtown. I walked down familiar elm-shaded streets and through empty lots I had traversed since I was fourteen. That was the year we moved to San Juan, refugees from Colorado snow and hard times. I saw so many people I had known in the old days, and they all knew about the baby. My father had been everywhere these past weeks, spreading the news. From front porches they shouted their good wishes, asking of Joyce, for she was a native of San Juan; her parents were buried in the local graveyard. People stopped me on the street, pumped my hand, made schmaltzy jokes, and went away laughing. Fatherhood was a very impressive business in San Juan. I had a rare sense of importance. Down in Los

Angeles they worried too, not about the wife and baby, but about your ability to pay hospital bills. Our friends were more shocked than pleased when they learned Joyce was pregnant.

For two hours I loafed around. I drank beer at the Tuscany Club, and shot a game of pool with Reed Walker at the Sylvan Oaks. Reed was postmaster; he had been Joyce's beau in high school. Not one person I met that afternoon was unaware of the coming child, not even Lou Sing, down in the faded brick buildings that comprised San Juan's Chinatown. We sat in front of Lou's herb shop and played chess, his many children shouting and playing in the street. At seven o'clock it was still daylight. The marquee lights went on at the San Juan Theater.

Suddenly I was imbued with the spirit of Joyce, lonely for her. The town had done it, the knowing that she had played in these streets as a little girl, and I was full of quick obscure desire. I went to a pay station and telephoned her long distance. I told her my mission had been a failure, that I was coming home as soon as possible. She asked of the town, how it looked.

"Remember the pepper tree in Mother's back yard?" she asked. "Is it still there? Have they cut it down?" I told her I'd walk over and find out.

"My first doll is buried under that tree. She died of knife wounds — scalped by the Indians."

"A horrible death."

"Her head was all broken in. The dog did it. I cried and cried."

I hung up and walked down Lincoln Street to the place Joyce had lived as a child. The house had been torn down years ago, and the city now used the land for parking bulldozers, scrapers and street-repair equipment. The pepper tree was still there. I stood under it, touched the trunk. I was very lonely for my wife. Ants crawled in the bark of the tree. I picked off two small red ants and put them in my mouth and chewed and swallowed them. Then I walked back to Mama's house.

§ § §

Papa wasn't there. The table was set in the kitchen — plates for three of us. Seated at the window, Mama was reciting the rosary. Twilight dimmed the room. She smiled without speaking, indicating that she had spoken to Papa. I waited for her to finish the beads. Dinner warmed on the stove: liver and bacon, peas cooked in onion, spinach and cheese. I sampled everything, drank a glass of wine, and waited. She told the last bead, kissed the cross, and put the rosary in her apron pocket.

"What'd he say?"

"Nothing. Not a word. He just walked out."

"Where is he?"

She rolled her eyes and rocked her head. Papa was on the town, drinking to forget his troubles.

"I don't blame him, Mama."

"He took ten dollars."

"What's the difference?"

"He'll drink brandy. He'll spend it all."

"Good. He has it coming."

"Oh, I'm not worried. I said the rosary. He'll be all right. But he'll spend ten dollars."

I took out my wallet and gave her five new twenty-dollar bills.

"I can't take it," she said. "You'll need it for the baby."
She folded the money and put it inside her blouse. "I really
shouldn't take it. I don't know what's come over me." I knew
of course what would happen to that hundred. The moment
I left town she would air mail it to my brother Jim, who
was having a rough time in Susanville.

She served my dinner. She had me alone, all to
herself, and I prepared for it, feeling it coming on. Sure
enough, she began making passes at me, those mother-passes
that leave you helpless. She stood behind me and touched
my hair. She fondled my ears. She let her arms drop over
my shoulders, her palms rubbing my chest. I kept reaching
for things, extricating myelf from every new hold. She finally took my left hand and began exploring the fingers. I tried
tugging it away, gently, but she would not let go, kissing
each finger. I felt great pity for her, for all women with their
great consuming mother passion. Then she found a little
mark on my neck where a cat had scratched me as a boy,
and this brought a fresh facet of her loneliness, and she hurried to the trunk in the bedroom, and I knew it was coming, a picture of me at six months, popeyed and naked on
a velvet pedestal. I jumped up from the table.

"Please, Mama. For God's sake, not that."

She put the picture away and began clearing the
table. I drank wine, watched the clock on the stove, and
read the *Sacramento Bee*. Mama took a colander of scraps
out to the chicken yard. Pretty soon she was back with three
egs. One in particular she singled out and brought to me
at the table.

"Feel. It's warm, from the mother hen."

I didn't want to feel it. Warm or cold, I wanted
nothing to do with it.

"Feel how nice and warm it is."

I wouldn't. I just stared at it. The egg stared back like a white oval eye, melancholy, stupid.

"They're good for you. Eat lots of them."

"Take it away. Put it some place else."

Time passed. I watched the clock and listened for footsteps in the yard. It was good to see my people again, but now I wanted to get away. Though I had plane reservations for the next day, and a ticket for Papa, I considered leaving that night. I had brought unhappiness to Papa. Best now to leave and let time and distance restore him.

Mama had unpacked my grip that afternoon. Now she began another inspection of the contents. She wanted to know the price of everything. I had brought an extra pair of slacks. She carried them out of the closet and flung them on the table. She examined the cuffs, the seat, the zipper. There was a food spot in front. With an exclamation she discovered this spot.

"What on earth do you suppose it is?"

"Don't worry about it, Mama. Just put it away."

She spread the trousers on the table and made a production out of it. She got a small cloth and soap and water and began scrubbing the place.

"I wonder what it is."

"Please, Mama. Leave it alone."

"It won't come off."

She kept probing around. I leaped out of the chair and took the trousers away from her.

"I'll send them to the cleaners."

"That costs money."

"I don't care."

"Doesn't Joyce look after your clothes?"

"Of course."

"Sending them to the cleaners — that's the American style."

I went out on the front porch and sat in the moonlight. The stars floated low and cool. Thirty miles to the east shone the Sierra snows, star-stuff, distant and lonely. A passenger plane droned through the sky, green and red lights blinking. I was homesick for my wife, and worried about my father. It was ten o'clock. There was a midnight plane out of Sacramento for the South. I made a decision: I would find Papa, bring him home, and take that plane.

Then this car with feeble headlights came clattering down the road. It was Joe Muto's old Ford. Joe was driving. He pulled up in front of the house. I went down to the fence and we greeted one another.

"You look for your father?" he said.

"Have you seen him?"

"On my land. Now. I think he have too much to drink."

I climbed into the truck and he turned it around. We went bumping down the broken road I had traveled that afternoon with my father.

"I hear him in there," Joe said. "He feel pretty bad."

We descended the small hill where the road turned left until we came to the section of uncultivated land. Joe stopped the car and I jumped out. Everything was clear in the moonlight. A community of bullfrogs and crickets filled the air with mating calls. Then I saw my father. He was sitting under one of the old lemon trees, a bottle in his hand. If he saw me, he paid no attention. Joe Muto stayed in the car and I went forward through the whistling weeds.

My father was talking to himself.

"Don't you worry about your Grandpa. He's not so old like they think. You'll get your house, little boy. Your Grandpa, he's not dead yet. Everybody tries to kill an old man, but your Grandpa ain't through yet."

I clenched my teeth to hold back the pain.

"Papa."

He saw me before him and cast the bottle aside in the weeds. Then he turned his head to the tree and wept in gusts of bitterness. I could not move toward him. Joe called from the car, asking if all was well. I waded through the weeds, back to the road.

"He's all right. I'll get him home okay."

"You have fight with your old man?"

"You go ahead. No fight. Thanks."

He drove away. I sat down at the side of the road to wait, lighting a cigarette. I was helpless. After about twenty minutes my father came plowing through the weeds. He knew I was there. He was not surprised to see me.

"Let's go home," he said.

He was sober, sighing heavily as his feet touched the road. In silence we walked side by side. The night was warm and sweet. To the north glowed the huge gold dome of the state capitol. It was set in a red haze rising out of the city lights.

"How you feel, Papa?"

"Me? I'm used to it. Some day you'll be old, and you'll have sons—thirty-five years from now, forty. You remember what your Papa said tonight: they hurt you every time."

"It's too bad."

For a while he didn't say any more. We neared the

house. The light was on, showing the front porch. We could see Mama, a shawl around her shoulders, looking for us.

"What's these termites doing in your house?" Papa said.

"You know — termites."

"Didn't you have the house inspected before you bought it?"

I told him about it. "Could you come down, Papa? You could help us. I got tickets for you on the plane."

"No plane for me. No, sir."

"Will you come, Papa? We'll take the train."

"Train, yes. Plane, no."

"Fine, Papa. Wonderful."

§   §   §

So he was coming to fix my house. I wanted Mama to come too, but she decreed that she should stay home and mind the cats and chickens. She was really glad, for trains filled her with dread. Only once in her life had she traveled by rail. That was in the summer of 1912, a thirty-five-mile honeymoon excursion from Denver to Colorado Springs. Our family didn't reach California by train. We loaded all we could haul into Papa's truck and rambled straight out Highway 40 until we got to San Juan.

My father, however, was an experienced railroad traveler. As far back as 1910 he had had train experience, coming out to Colorado from New York by rail, traversing the entire distance in a railroad coach. Nor was this the end of his rail travels. Three years later, alone, he boarded a narrow-gauge train from Denver to Boulder, a distance of thirty miles. Following this, he made the honeymoon jaunt to Colorado Springs with Mama. With such a background, he exhibited a fine fearlessness about trains. Frequently now—two or three times a year—he swung aboard a Sacramento local for trips to the state capital and back. Trains held no fear whatever for this man.

The Los Angeles train—the West Coaster—left Sacramento at six every evening. We decided at breakfast to take the next train. I borrowed my brother-in-law's car and drove to Sacramento to make arrangements. I cancelled the plane reservations and got space on that evening's West Coaster. The train was almost solidly booked, but I managed to get a section for us on the Pullman. I wanted the old man to be comfortable, and I made sure he had a lower berth.

An hour before train time I was back in San Juan. Stella was there with her children and Steve, her husband. Papa was dressed and ready to go. He wore an odd assortment of things: blue overalls with a bib, a black shirt topped by a white tie, and a double-breasted brown coat. I recognized the coat as part of a suit I had given him the year before. In fact, he had a large wardrobe of his sons' suits and topcoats, for we were of the same measurements as he. Certainly he had four or five suits of clothes, any one of which would have been fine for travel.

"Why the overalls?" I asked.

He glanced at himself.

"What's wrong with them?"

"Don't you have the pants to that suit?"

"Don't like 'em."

He sat at the kitchen table, his face shaved and powdered, his hair neatly parted. His bull neck under the black shirt looked puffy from the strain of the white tie.

Yet he had that distinguished appearance of a man about to embark on a long journey.

Stella said, "He's stubborn. He doesn't want to look nice and clean."

"I *am* clean. What I got on is clean and just washed."

"But overalls! On the train."

"I rode trains before you was born. So don't tell your Papa about trains."

"No use going around like an old bricklayer."

"What's wrong with laying brick?"

"How about that gray suit?" I suggested. "It might be cooler on the train."

He got to his feet with a reddened angry face.

"You want me to come down? You want me to help you with the house?"

I certainly did.

"Then don't tell me what to wear. You ain't so smart, and don't forget it. Buying a house with termites!"

That ended the matter. I didn't want to lose him.

His luggage was piled near the door, two paint-scarred suitcases of imitation leather tied with clothesline, and a canvas mason's kit. Meanwhile Mama kept out of the discussion, busying herself putting things into a grocer's carton that once held canned milk. I went over to see what she was doing. She was packing this stuff for me to take back to Los Angeles. The box contained four quarts of home-canned tomato preserves and four quarts of fig jelly. There was also a head of goat's cheese and a freshly baked chocolate cake.

"They don't have good cake in Los Angeles," she said.

I could not imagine how she came upon this information, but I didn't say anything. Now she showed me a small bouquet of sweet basil freshly cut from her herb garden, and tied with a red ribbon from which hung two lead medals of the Blessed Virgin Mary.

"It's to make the baby born alive. Every night, hang it at the foot of your bed."

I said I would do this.

Papa came forward with a coil of clothesline and began tying the carton. Mama drew me to the sink for a little confidential talk. She opened a drawer filled with spices and drew out a garlic clove. With her fingernail she peeled the clove naked and white. Then she kissed it and shoved it into the lapel pocket of my coat.

"Keep some in your pocket all the time, day and night. Never be without it."

"I know. It makes boys."

She smiled tolerantly, shrugging her hands.

"Me—I don't care. Boy or girl, he's my grandchild. I'll love him just the same. But your Papa wants a boy. It's to please him, the garlic."

The fierce fumes of the garlic stabbed my nostrils, and I knew I would have to dump the bulb as soon as possible or it would pervade my clothes. Now it was time to leave. Steve and Papa carried the luggage to the car. I distinctly heard the glub-glub of wine bottles in one of the grips. Mama didn't see me remove the garlic from my pocket and flip it into the grape hedge. She went down to the car with me. Because of the children, she and Stella weren't going to the station with us.

Papa kissed the two little girls, and then Mama, and he cried a little, telling her not to forget to put a bit of parsley in the cat's food during the hot weather. Mama was being brave and fighting off collapse as we embraced and kissed good-by. Steve turned the car around, honking the horn as we waved, and then Mama collapsed. She sank neatly to the road beside the fence as the car rolled away. Stella was there beside her, quite unperturbed, waving to us, and Mama looked thoroughly insensible, her head on her breast, her hand struggling bravely to wave at us, and finally floundering in the dust. We should have stopped to "revive" her, but time was short, and Papa was anxious to make contact with the train.

"Nothing wrong with her. Let's go."

We turned the corner and the tires hummed evenly on the fine highway toward Sacramento. I sighed with relief and reached for a cigarette. My hand came upon something warm and sticky in my pocket. I pulled out a clove of garlic. It lay in my hand, naked and white and ferocious. I would have thrown it away but Papa was looking at it too.

"Good," he said. "Now you're talking. I got mine too."

He took out a coin purse with many compartments. In one of these lay a clove of garlic. My brother-in-law saw it too.

"That don't work," Steve said. "Stella and I tried it — twice."

THREE

IT WAS MY first train ride with Papa, and it proved to be a nightmare. From the moment we said good-by to Steve and entered the depot, there were difficulties. We had five pieces of luggage: Papa's tool kit, his two crummy suitcases, the roped carton of home preserves, and my overnight bag. The tool kit alone weighed fifty pounds, for it was loaded with chisels, hammers and other hunks of steel used in the trade. Three redcaps saw us struggling under this gear and rushed forward with generous hands. I produced our tickets and one of them began writing out claim checks. Papa was astonished.

"What's going on? What they want?"

"He'll take this stuff to our car."

"You have to pay? How much?"

Fifty cents seemed reasonable.

"You crazy? I'll do it myself, for nothing."

"Look, Papa. This is the way it's done. It's miles to the train."

He wouldn't have it. He ordered the redcap to move on. "I got two jugs of wine in that black one. He might break it."

"I'll be very careful, sir," the redcap said.

"Nothing doing."

"Please, Papa. At least let him haul that tool kit."

"I got a trowel in there, she's forty years old. Them tools cost me two hundred dollars."

"Whatever you say, Mister," the redcap smiled.

I thanked him. "We'll manage," I said. "Here."

I flipped him a quarter. He snatched it out of the air, grinned and backed off. Papa blinked, unbelieving.

"You give him money? What for?"

"He's got to eat too."

He went running after the redcap, yelling at him to come back, come back here, you. The redcap returned, startled and smiling. Papa pointed to the grips.

"Carry them — all but this." He shook one of the roped suitcases, heard the low glub-glub laughter of bottled wine, and seemed satisfied. The redcap wrote out claim checks for the other pieces and loaded them into the baggage wagon. Papa supervised the operation.

"Don't lose them tools. I got a level in there cost me twenty dollars."

"I'll be very careful, sir."

It left Papa dubious. "I had trouble with them fellows when I come out from New York."

We went down into the passenger subway and drifted along with a river of travelers flowing toward the trains. It was a leisurely walk, with ten minutes remaining before our West Coaster departed. Suddenly half a dozen sailors came pounding down the subway, running hard to catch the San Francisco Limited. Their agitation was contagious and many who walked now began running too. One of these was Papa. Suitcase swinging, he went pattering down the runway, calling me to come on, hurry up. I picked up the pace, but it was not fast enough for him. In the distance I saw him reach our train and try to get aboard at the first open door. A brakeman detained him. They were in a fierce argument when I came up, the brakeman insisting that he knew our car number and Papa equally emphatic that it didn't make any difference. Ours was Car 21, far to the rear. All the way back Papa kept mumbling about the stupidity of train operations, how things had changed since his New York trip, changed for the worse.

"Car Twenty-one. Car Eighty-one. What's the difference? There's only one train, and the whole thing goes to Los Angeles."

I tried to explain, but he cut me short.

"Son, I rode trains before you was born. Before I even *met* your mother. Are you gonna tell me about trains?"

We climbed aboard Car 21. The redcap arrived at the same time, sweat oozing from his brown face as he wrestled with the tool kit. Papa sat down and lit a cigar. Immediately the porter for Car 21 came over and told him there was no smoking except in the men's washroom. With a scowl, Papa heeled out his cigar.

"What kind of a train *is* this, anyhow?"

"Men's washroom at the end of the car," the porter said. He was in his late sixties, with white hair and much wrinkling about the eyes. Now the redcap was back with the rest of the luggage. He wiped the sweat from his face, and his tongue hung out.

"You need a drink," Papa said.

"Never turn down a drink," the redcap laughed.

Quickly Papa unroped the black suitcase and flung it open. There were two gallon jugs of claret wrapped in towels. There was a third sack, bulging with stuff. I looked inside. It held two loaves of round homemade bread and a goat's cheese the size of a football. At the bottom of the sack was a foot-long salami and a quantity of apples and oranges.

"What's this for?"

"You got to eat," he answered sharply.

The redcap roared with laughter.

"That's right. Man's got to eat on the train."

It pleased Papa. Redcap wasn't such a bad fellow, after all. He grinned, his face purpling as he tried to unscrew the cap on the wine jug. "I seen you some place before," he said. "You ever carry a hod around Denver, Colorado, in 1922, '23?"

Redcap was delighted.

"Not me — no sir! Rassling baggage is all I'm good for."

Papa got the cap off the jug. As he handed it to Redcap the towel fell away, and the jug suddenly loomed up, dark red and shocking, like a bomb. Redcap was startled.

"Maybe we better go back to the smoker."

Papa followed him to the end of the car, the jug like a baby in his arms, and they darted inside the men's room. Car 21 was rapidly filling. People in the aisle turned frowning faces on the open suitcase, the roped carton, the tool kit smeared with mortar. No doubt about it: all that gear took a lot of glamour out of Car 21 and there was good reason for the disapproval of the others. Back in the men's room I could hear Redcap howling with laughter. I closed the suitcase and decided to go back too.

Redcap was introducing Papa to our porter.

"You gentlemen gonna see lots of one another. Mr. Randolph, allow me to present my good friend, Mr. Fante."

Papa shook hands.

"Randolph?" he said. "Randolph? You ever carry a hod, Mr. Randolph? Up in Boulder, Colorado, 1916, 1917?"

"Nineteen-sixteen? No, sir. Had a cousin, though. And *he* carried a hod. Down in Montgomery, Alabama. Long time ago."

"That's the fellow," Papa said. "I thought so."

Redcap was howling with laughter again. Mr. Randolph drank long and expertly from the jug, tilting it from his raised elbow. He smacked his lips and handed it to Papa, who pulled at it lovingly. Then he passed it to Redcap.

"Mr. Randolph," Papa began. "The trouble with the white people in this country . . ."

But he got no further, for I had suddenly had enough of his antics. There was no harm in having a drink with your fellow man, but there was a time and place for everything, and the spectacle of this old man in overalls gallivanting up and down a railway car with a gallon of wine and feting the hired hands seemed to be carrying things too far. Besides, he didn't *have* to wear overalls.

I pulled him back to our section as the train began to move out of Sacramento. He was humiliated and taciturn. He put one jug back in the grip, but he kept the other in readiness under the seat. By now everyone in the car, well-dressed men and women, were aware of the red jug that bobbed into view each time he took a drink.

"Children—bah," he muttered.

"Hate their father . . ."

"Ashamed of their own flesh and blood . . ."

"Better to die. Bury you. Forget you . . ."

"Worked hard all my life. My own flesh and blood abuse me . . ."

"Ready to go any time. Done my duty . . ."

"When you're old, they throw you out . . ."

His voice carried. He had it pitched high enough to reach most ears. All around me I felt the smouldering of the others, the heads turning, the shocked stares at me, the pity for my old man. Mr. Randolph didn't help matters. With touching solicitude he brought Papa a pillow, smiled tenderly, asked how Papa was getting along.

"You take it easy now, Mr. Fante. Have a nice trip. Anything you want, just ring the bell. You got friends on this train. Lots of friends."

Tears stung Papa's eyes.

"I try to get along, Mr. Randolph. I don't want to make no trouble for anybody. Lots of nice people on the train. Fine ladies and gentlemen. I do my best."

I chewed my fingernails and kept still. A waiter came through the car sounding dinner chimes. It brightened the moment. I slapped Papa on the shoulder.

"Come on, Papa. Let's have a nice dinner."

"I'm all right, son. You go. I don't want to cause you no more trouble. I got my own dinner right here. Try to save you a little money, son."

One thing was certain: I didn't want salami, goat's cheese, bread and wine for dinner. Earlier my thought had been a couple of dry Martinis, a steak and a good salad. Now I only wanted a cup of black coffee and the chance to get away for a while. A dozen pairs of cold eyes watched me grope down the aisle toward the diner, four cars away.

The distance was magic. My appetite returned. I had two Manhattans and a small steak. By the time the train pulled out of Stockton I felt fine again, lingering for a second cup of coffee. Darkness had come. One by one the little San Joaquin Valley towns flew past, each like the other bejeweled in city lights. The manager of the diner brought my check. I reached into my pocket and pulled out a soft white object among the coins. It was another garlic clove. It had a savage pungency, clean and caustic. I dropped it into a glass of water.

As I rose to leave, the conductor came through the car, collecting tickets. He examined mine.

"Oh," he said. "You're the old man's son."

"He didn't want any dinner," I blurted. "I mean, he had his dinner with him."

He was tight-lipped, noncommittal. He removed the stubs and handed the tickets back to me. His eyes were as cold as oysters.

"Honor thy father and thy mother," he said.

"I don't like goat's cheese."

His lips curled. He hated me.

Back in Car 21, Papa was breaking their hearts. I found him partaking of a simple repast of bread, cheese and salami, and washing it down with occasional sips of wine. He ate with mincing delicacy, a gentleman at table. His pocketknife lay open in his lap, and his food was spread across the opposite seat. Mr. Randolph had provided a napkin, and he hovered in the aisle, listening with gentle eyes as Papa spoke. He was talking about the hard bitter days of his youth back in Abruzzi; how he had gone to work at the age of ten, apprenticed to a cruel stonemason who cheated him of his wages of three cents a day; how his own mother used to come to the job and help him carry big stones up a ladder to the scaffolding on the estate of the Duke of Abruzzi. It was a tragic story, and a true story, for I had heard it many times before; had been raised on it, in fact;

a tale of peasant misery that turned one's blood to tears, and those near him in Car 21 were deeply moved by the words of this simple old man who found contentment in a bit of bread and cheese and salami while his son gorged himself riotously on rich foods.

I sat down beside him, hunched my shoulders, and wished I'd worn a hat to hide my face. Papa's humble voice, rich now with gratitude, went out to Mr. Randolph and everybody else.

"But God Almighty's been good to me. I'm an American citizen. Been one for twenty-five years. I got four fine children. I raised them and sent them out into this great country of ours. She's a wonderful place, this America. She's been good to all of us. God bless the United States of America."

A large man in tweeds across the aisle now leaned toward us and offered Papa a cigar. It was an expensive cigar, packed in a bullet-shaped humidor. With a simple dignity Papa accepted it, bowing from the waist.

"Thank you, Mister. I'll save it for when my grandson's born. She's too good to smoke now."

It was very touching. The man in tweeds looked to his big blond wife, whose bosom heaved, whose face was framed in tenderness. She whispered something, and the man in tweeds now produced a second cigar. Papa protested that this was too much, too much, but he let them force it upon him. Mr. Randolph urged him to go back to the men's room and enjoy the gift, and Papa agreed. Carefully he put away his bread, wrapped his salami in a dishcloth, and tucked up his goat's cheese in a sack. Not one crumb was wasted. He closed the suitcase and got to his feet. He was tight, but it took an experienced filial eye to notice it.

72

Mr. Randolph assisted him dowr the aisle. Heads turned to watch him go. He left a trail of love in his wake.

I leaned against the window and stared straight ahead. I was very lonely and friendless. Papa's absence created an hiatus distinctly felt. The train pounded ahead. The man in tweeds and his wife rose to go to the diner. I was not worthy of his glance, but his wife looked down at me with flaring nostrils. Mr. Randolph returned.

"The old gentleman wishes his black suitcase."

I handed Mr. Randolph two garlic-scorched dollars.

"See that he gets whatever he wants."

"Don't you worry about that."

He sniffed the garlic and looked at me suspiciously.

A few minutes later he was back in the car, making up the berths. I went into the men's room. Papa sat red-eyed at the window, mumbling to himself. The room was full of expensive cigar smoke.

"The berths are being made, Papa. You better go to bed."

"Go on, son. Have a good time. Laugh and play, don't worry about your father."

"I think you ought to go to bed."

"Not me. No train beds for Nick Fante. I'll stay right here."

And there he stayed. I went back to the club car and had a brandy. When I returned to Car 21 Mr. Randolph had made up all the berths. The men's room was crowded, passengers washing their faces, scrubbing teeth, preparing to retire. Everybody called my father "Dad" and wished him good night. Nobody had a word for me. I gritted my teeth and brazened it out, smoking cigarettes and gasping for tomorrow morning, when the black journey would come to an end.

By eleven o'clock all the passengers in Car 21 were in bed except Papa and me. He slept by the window, snoring. I shook him awake.

"Come to bed."

"No, sir."

"You can't sleep here. I got a nice bed for you."

"No, sir."

Mr. Randolph entered.

"Poor old fellow. He's so tired."

"He won't sleep in a berth."

"Mighty fine old man."

"Help me get him to bed."

We tried to lift him, but he kicked with such energy, and he was wearing heavy work shoes, that it was useless. I pleaded and argued.

"No, sir."

It defeated me. I went down to our section and got into the lower berth. Since Papa refused to stretch out, I saw no reason for climbing into the upper. I had trouble sleeping. The berth was hot and stifling. Three times I rose, pulled on my pants and went down to the men's room. Papa lay full length on the seat. Each time I shook him, he growled and started kicking. I went back to my berth. It was choked with heat. I rang for Mr. Randolph. He was asleep in a lower near the men's room. He had little patience with me.

"It's too hot in there," I said. "Close up the upper berth so I can get some air."

He did as I asked. Now I had the whole section opened up and it felt much better when I lay down. In a little while I was asleep.

It was morning when I awoke. The train was leaving

Castaic in the mountains and we were a little more than an hour out of Los Angeles. I dressed with wonderful freedom, for I could stand up now that the upper had been closed. Then I stepped into the aisle. Every other passenger was awake and dressed. Every berth save mine had been made up. Mr. Randolph busied himself with a whisk broom. All eyes were upon me. If these people disliked me the night before, they were now ready to lynch me. Their animosity was like a stultifying hot wind, unmistakable and frightening. Then I realized what it was that angered them. The berth above me was closed; it had been unused through the night. Only the lower had been occupied, and by none other than myself. Papa, they knew, was in the men's room. The implication was wretchedly obvious: while I slept in luxurious ease, occupying the space allotted for two people, my poor old father had been forced to spend the night in the men's washroom. With a tight jaw I staggered down the aisle, ten miles through hostile Indian country, to the men's smoker.

And there was Papa. He had the black suitcase open in his lap, and he was eating a simple breakfast of goat's cheese and apples. The man in tweeds stood over him.

"You sleep well, Dad?"

Papa's smile implied that he hadn't slept too well, but well enough under the circumstances. I wanted to cut out his heart, and the man in tweeds wanted to cut out mine.

Not until we reached Los Angeles, until we were away from his loyal train comrades, until he had shaken hands with all of them and bade a fond good-by, not until then did I have my revenge. Our luggage had been checked through to the taxi stand outside the Los Angeles Union Station. In grim silence we walked down the passenger subway and through the depot to the taxi stand. I gave a redcap our claim stubs and he pulled the luggage off a hand truck. Papa had his coin purse out, ready to offer a tip. A thin dime was poised between his thumb and forefinger.

"Don't take his money," I told the redcap.

He was only too glad not to, seeing the dime. Then I knew how I would have my revenge. I pulled out my wallet and slowly counted out five one-dollar bills into the palm of the grinning redcap. Papa watched in unbelief, his tongue out.

"What's going on?"

Redcap beamed. "Thank you!"

I hailed a cab. Papa looked around, stunned, expecting something unusual to happen for five dollars, but the redcap walked away counting the money. A cab drew up. The driver piled our luggage into the front seat. Still Papa stood there, waiting for some kind of action. The redcap drifted away through the throng.

"What happened? Where's he going?"

"Let's go, Papa."

"You have change back coming."

"I gave it all to him."

"You crazy?"

Before I could stop him, he was running after the redcap, jostling the others, fighting his way through the crowd, yelling, "Mister! Hey, Mister! Come back."

But the redcap was gone, devoured in the swirl of people hurrying to and from the trains. Papa stood crestfallen, almost in tears, his quick eyes darting everywhere.

"He's gone. He took your money."

"I wanted him to have it."

He swung around, his hands exhorting me, his face purpling with anger. "You don't know what you're doing. Money's hard to get. You need it — every penny — to buy shoes, to buy milk and bread. For your wife, for the baby."

Aye, he was right, my Papa. Mine had been the vengeance of a fool. Too soon I had forgotten the lean years that were past, the lean years that were surely coming again. We walked back to the taxi. I got in. Papa hesitated at the door.

"How much it cost?"

"Not much, Papa. A few cents."

He climbed in and I explained how the meter determined the amount of the fare. I gave the driver our address and he pushed the lever setting the meter in motion. The cab moved out of the Union Station. The meter showed the minimum fare.

"It's only twenty cents," Papa smiled. He sat back, satisfied. We moved up Aliso to Los Angeles Street, the first block signal. There was a sharp click and the meter jumped to thirty cents.

"What's going on?"

"Take it easy, Papa. We got about eight miles to go. It won't cost much."

He leaned forward in his seat. The streets of the city, the downtown throngs, had no interest. Only the meter held his attention. We reached Main Street. I pointed to the massive City Hall. The meter clicked.

"It's forty cents," he said.

We moved into Spring Street, with the Plaza not far away, and the Los Angeles tenderloin. Not many years ago I had walked these streets lonely and penniless. I had slept in the Sunshine Mission and snipped cigarette butts from the sand jugs in front of elevator shafts. There were days when I walked around without socks. Once I had been a bus boy in Simon's on Hill Street, hosing out garbage cans, polishing brass rails. Those days had long since lost their appeal. I was glad to be away from cheap Temple Street hotels, two-cent coffee, and shaves in public lavatories with cold water and old razor blades. There had been days on those downtown streets when a single dollar bill in my pocket meant a time to relax from the fever of keeping alive, a time to slacken the pace, to take it easy for twenty-four hours. We passed Pershing Square. The meter clicked. Papa mopped his face with a large blue handkerchief.

"She's up to seventy cents. Let's get out."

Beyond the Square was the all-night movie house where, for a dime, I used to sleep until five in the morning. Then they kicked us out, and I always used the fire exits, but the rubes staggered sleepily through the front door to be grabbed by cops and hauled off to Lincoln Heights Jail on a vagrancy charge. Once it had happened to me, and it could happen again, unless I worked hard, unless I took Papa's advice and saved my money. The cab cruised up Seventh Street, the meter clicking every now and then, with Papa getting more and more panicky as the figures mounted.

Pretty soon it got to me too, and I began to stare at that meter, frightened and fascinated. When we swung into Wilshire Boulevard it was nearly two dollars, and I was sweating it out with Papa. I had over a hundred dollars in my wallet but I was thinking about the old days, the desperate urgency of thrift now that the baby was coming, the irrevocable loss of pennies wasted. When the meter reached two dollars, Papa groaned in pain, swaying his head.

"How much we got to go?"

"A mile or two."

It was more than that. I had taken the trip by cab before and it was a five-dollar fare, or thereabouts, and it seemed fabulous now, too dear for such as I. We traveled on a few blocks more, and suddenly I could not bear it. I pounded the glass separating us from the driver.

"Stop this cab. Right here."

Instantly he pulled over to the curb.

"You ain't there yet, bub."

"This is as far as we go."

"That's your privilege."

He tore the price ticket out of the meter. It was $3.20. I paid it to the penny, no more and no less. The driver piled our luggage on the sidewalk and drove away. Let him sneer! A penny saved was a penny earned. Today it was fashionable to scoff at the homely wisdom of a Carnegie or a Rockefeller. I saw now that those great men were right.

"Let's go, Papa. It's not far. Only a couple of miles."

He spat on his hands.

"Now you're talking, boy."

All credit were credit is due. But for Papa I might have been ground under, to fall there in some hot and unclean gutter, never to see my Joyce again. But for him the safari might have ended in complete demoralization, Mama's heavy jars of tomato and fig preserves and an uncut chocolate cake abandoned along the trail.

His was the strength of ten as we slugged along, the madness of the heat twisting my reason, the choking fumes of monoxide gas burning my parched lips. He carried his tool kit in one hand, a suitcase in the other, and a third suitcase under his arm. Twenty paces behind, I fought through beneath the awful weight of the roped carton and my own grip. Unflinchingly he bore the hardships of that desperate trek, calling out words of encouragement to the younger man who wanted to quit before every drugstore that wafted its aroma of ice-cold cola and chocolate soda. But a penny saved was a penny earned. I was in this thing to the bitter end. I was a goddamned fool and I knew it.

At last we reached the house. Papa was fresh as a bull. I threw myself on the lawn. From the window Joyce saw us and rushed out. One look at her, the lush roundness of her waist, and Papa dropped his luggage and began to cry. He held out his arms.

"Ah, Miss Joyce! The baby, he's beautiful."

"Papa Fante!"

She ran to meet him, her arms out, looped around his neck, the soft pressure of the bulge against his waist, so that he backed away discreetly, but she clung to him and he was embarrassed and awed by the wonderful balloon.

"We're so glad you came," she smiled. "We need you very much."

He laughed and patted her clumsily, adoring her and the voluptuous roundness that contained a part of him too. You could see him tremble before it, giddy with joy, this extension of himself, the projection of his life far beyond the limits of his years upon the earth. Sitting on the grass and watching him, I knew suddenly that even the birth of his own children had not held the romance and excitement of this child's coming. Over his shoulder Joyce looked down at me with startled eyes. I just sat there, glad to be home, too tired to speak.

"John . . . what happened?"

"We walked."

I got up and we kissed.

"Why didn't you take a cab?"

"We did that too."

I did not wish to discuss the matter further. I wanted a bath, some clean clothes and a chance to go on living, to forget that black passage. Papa was kicking the lawn with the thick toe of his shoe.

"Devil grass. All devil grass. No good, this country."

His gaze followed two lanes of tall palms marching down both sides of the avenue, their sleek trunks soaring, their fronds like feather dusters on long handles.

"No good, them trees. No shade, no fruit, no nothing."

We gathered the luggage and carried it into the house, piling it in the hall before the staircase. To the left of the hall, and one step down, was the living room, with wide French windows and cool green walls, a large pleasant room with a beige carpet and carefully selected white oak pieces. Standing there, I felt again that it was a good house in spite of the hole in the kitchen floor; yes, a fine house, a happy house, and it made me proud to be the owner, and I put my arm around Joyce.

"Here she is, Papa. My house."

He turned his head here and there as he bit off the end of a fresh cigar, struck a match against his thigh, and lit up.

"Floor ain't plumb."

"Oak floor, Papa. Very good floor."

"Ain't plumb."

We looked down at the floor. It seemed flawless.

"Tool kit," he said again.

His kit was piled with the other things.

"Tool kit," he said again.

"It's right here."

"Tool kit," he repeated.

It was several moments before I realized what he meant — that I should open his tool kit. Even as I became aware of this, I knew that the man had taken over, that our relationship had suddenly changed, that he was the boss of the job. I remembered it from a long time ago when I lived under his roof with my brothers and worked as his helper on building jobs. It was the worst part of working for this man, and we never liked it, my brothers and I. In those days he would say, "Pencil," and it meant: give me a pencil. Or he would say: "Two-by-four, three feet long." It was a part of the mystery of working for him, because he never explained why he wanted the thing. He never explained anything, and we used to walk off the job in a fury of frustration and anger, because he treated us like slaves. And here it was again, after sixteen years, this man standing in my house and saying, "Tool kit."

I unbuckled the kit and pulled it open.

"Half-inch pipe. Foot long."

I burrowed at the bottom of the kit and found several pieces of pipe. He paced back and forth studying the floor. I gave him what he wanted. But he only glanced at it and did not take it.

"Wrong pipe."

"That's what you asked for."

"Half-inch pipe. Foot long."

I dug into the kit and found another. It seemed right. I held it out.

"Wrong pipe."

I flung it back, dug out all the short pieces of pipe

in the kit, and held them out. Quickly he took the one he wanted.

"Level."

I handed him the level.

He put it on the floor, got down on his knees, and studied the air bubble inside the measuring area.

"Tape measure."

I gave it to him, and he measured from the door to the first step of the staircase.

"Twelve foot."

He placed the pipe on the floor at the door, holding it with his foot. "Floor sags two inches. Pipe's gonna roll clear to the stairs. Whole house sags in the middle."

He took his foot off the pipe and it began to move, slowly at first, but quickly gaining speed as it clattered along; yea, even as it thumped against the stair I knew my Papa was the wrong man for the job; I knew that he hated the house, that he was prejudiced against it, that he would show it no mercy. We watched the pipe rocking back and forth and finally come to a stop. Joyce was stunned.

"For heaven's sake."

Papa picked up the length of pipe and handed it to me.

"Tool kit."

I threw the pipe into the kit.

"Lock."

I locked it.

"Straps."

I buckled the two straps.

"Termites," he said.

Joyce led him into the kitchen. I started up the stairs.

"Where you going?" he asked.

"Bath."

I went up and had my bath. For an hour I lay in warm soothing water, dozing but not sleeping. For me a bath was not so much the cleansing of the body as the refreshing of the mind. My thinking became like a summer sky, gladsome images crossing it like white clouds: the sailboats at Newport Beach, the haunting beauty of Valli, the third fairway at Fox Hills Golf Club, the prose of Willa Cather. All the delicious things, the winsome splendid gentle things, came with my bath.

But now something strange was added, a new and startling imagery, a pool of stagnant water, mossy and cool. Deep forest shadows shrouded the pool, and there were creatures just below the surface of the water, popping their heads out and disappearing again, and, each time they sank, something white and terrible trailed in the water after them. Gradually I recognized the creatures. They were Papa, and Joe Muto, and Mr. Randolph, and the man in tweeds. The white stringy things they dragged after them were umbilical cords. The creatures were so frightening I jumped out of the tub and quickly dressed.

FOUR

JOYCE WAS IN the living room reading, surrounded with books. I could see Papa in the back yard. He sat under a wide lawn umbrella, a wine jug on the steel table beside him, a cigar in his mouth as he stretched his legs and took his ease, studying the house.

"What did he say about the hole in the kitchen?"

"He wants to consider it," Joyce said.

"There's nothing to consider. Just fix the hole."

She closed the book. "Let him think about it. He's full of ideas."

"No matter what he thinks, the hole has to be fixed. It was a mistake to bring him down here. He's old and set in his ways. I predict trouble."

"That's not a very nice way to feel about your own father."

"I can't help it. He's turned into an eccentric."

"You should have thought of that before you asked him. The Fourth Commandment, you know."

"The Fourth Commandment?"

"Honor thy father and thy mother."

I gave her a quick look. She was a picture of enormous placidity, her great tummy sitting proudly on her lap like another person. It gave you the feeling you talked to two people. Behind her reading glasses the gray eyes were clear and beautiful. She sat with a dozen books around her, some on the coffee table, others piled beside her on the divan. She was reading Chesterton and Belloc and Thomas Merton and François Mauriac. There were books by Karl Adam, Fulton Sheen and Evelyn Waugh. I glanced at some of the titles: *The Spirit of Catholicism, The Faith of Our Fathers, The Idea of a University.* Some of these books were mine, out of a dusty box in the garage, but most were new and fresh from the bookstore. It was incredible to find her with such books, for she was a cold materialist; she belonged to a semantic group; nay, she was practically an atheist, with a hard scientific patience for facts.

"What you doing?"

"I'm thinking of making a change." She took off her reading glasses. "If God is all-good, why does He permit crippled children to be born?"

It frightened me at once.

"Is something wrong with the baby?"

"Of course not. I'm asking you a question."

"I don't know the answer."

She smiled with satisfaction.

"But I do."

"That's just wonderful."

"Don't you want to hear it?"

I couldn't take her seriously. It was but another whim of her pregnancy. Here was the same girl who liked chili sauce on her avocado salad. It would pass as soon as her figure returned. It was a whim. It had to be. I liked an atheistic wife. Her position made matters easy for me. It simplified a planned family. We had no scruples about contraceptives. Ours had been a civil marriage. We were not chained by religious tenets. Divorce was there, any time we wanted it. If she became a Catholic there would be all manner of complications. It was hard to be a good Catholic, very hard, and that was why I had left the Church. To be a good Catholic you had to break through the crowd and help Him pack the cross. I was saving the breakthrough for later. If she broke through I might have to follow, for she was my wife. No; this was a whim of hers, a passing fancy. It had to be.

"You'll get over it," I said. "Any calls?"

"Nothing important."

I phoned my secretary at the studio. My calls were routine. Somebody wanted to play golf, and somebody else wanted to play poker. My producer was in New York, and the front office was very quiet. It was a good time to proceed with arrangements about repairing the kitchen. There was lumber to buy, and Papa would probably need a helper. I walked out to the back yard and took a chair under the big umbrella. Papa sat quietly, his feet on the table. His jug was almost empty. He watched his cigar smoke climb into the branches of a small mock orange tree in the center of the yard.

"What do you think, Papa? Will it cost much?"

"My eyes hurt. No good, this country."

"Smog. You'll have to replace some of the joists."

"Did I ever tell you about my Uncle Mingo and the bandits?"

"Sure, lots of times. Will you need a helper on the job?"

"Brave man, my Uncle Mingo. He was an Andrilli, your Grandma's brother. They hang him right there in

JOHN FANTE

Abruzzi. The *carabinieri* . . . Two bullets in his shoulder.
They hang him anyway. His wife standing there, crying.
Sixty-one years ago. I seen it myself. Coletta Andrilli, pretty
woman."

He drank, the jug in both hands, his Adam's apple
rising and falling. He put down the jug and resumed his
pleasant thoughts. I told him there was a lumber yard not
far away. If he would compute the materials needed we
could drive over to the lumber yard that very day.

"I'm anxious to get started, Papa."

Papa spoke to his cigar: "He's anxious to get started.
I been here two hours. I'm tired. I don't sleep good on the
train, but he wants to get started."

I apologized. He was right, of course. I had been very
thoughtless. "Certainly, Papa. I don't mean to rush you.
Take it easy for a few days. Get a good rest. The kitchen
can wait."

"I'll take care of the kitchen, kid. You take care of
the writing."

His face showed fatigue, gray bristles at his chin, the
tips of his mouth turned down, his eyes half open and bloodshot, smarting from the poison gas in the air.

"Enjoy yourself, Papa. Rest. Anything you want —
just ask for it. You need more wine?"

"Don't worry about the wine, kid. I'll take care of
the wine."

"I'll order you some Chianti, Papa. Real Chianti.
Anything else?"

"Typewrite machine."

"I got a portable upstairs. But you can't type, Papa."

He studied his cigar. "You type. I talk."

It touched me. Only last evening he had left Mama,

88

and now he wanted to send her a little message. "That's fine, Papa. She'll be very happy."

"She's dead."

"Who?"

"Coletta Andrilli."

"I thought you wanted to write a letter to Mama."

"What for? I seen her yesterday. Good God, kid."

"Why the typewriter?"

"My Uncle Mingo and the bandits. We write the story. For the little boy, so he'll know about Uncle Mingo. Make him feel good, proud."

"Not today, Papa. We'll do it, but later."

"Today. Now."

"But why today?"

Fiercely he answered, frightened he answered: "Because I might die any time. Any minute."

"Some other time."

Quick pain smothered his face. Without a word he rose and walked very fast into the house. I saw him hurry through the living room without speaking to Joyce. He clambered up the stairs. As I reached the living room the door of the guest bedroom closed sharply. Joyce peered at me over her reading glasses.

"What did you do to that poor old man?"

"Nothing. He wants me to write a story about his Uncle Mingo."

"You refused, of course."

"I said, later."

"After Dorothy Lamour and the gypsies?"

"Don't be clever."

"It's wrong to treat your father like this. It's a sin. You know very well that you should reverence the aged, specially your parents. It's your sacred obligation before God."

Big and calm, she was. A big white rock, unperturbed as the breakers smashed against her. A tower of ivory, she was, a morning star, a rolling hill, a Boulder Dam.

"What's eating you, anyhow?"

"I can't allow you to abuse your father."

I groped around for an answer, but there was none. It shook me up because she was so sure of herself. She was a woman of infinite tact who rarely lashed out. I thought of apologizing to Papa, but that would trap me into a session with his Uncle Mingo. Not that I hated Uncle Mingo. I didn't hate Uncle Mingo. I vowed again that I would write his story, but I just didn't want to write the goddamn thing at that moment.

"I'm going to the studio."

She had resumed her reading. She looked up.

"What did you say?"

"I'm going to the studio."

"If God is all-good and all-knowing, why does He create certain souls He knows will suffer eternal damnation?"

"I don't know."

"But I do," she smiled.

"Isn't that just ducky."

I walked out to the garage and got into the car. It was twenty minutes to the studio, through heavy crosstown traffic, but I was glad for the snarl of cars and the hooting of busses. Here was the temper of our time. After the baby was born, Joyce would feel it again, the comfort of confusion, the all-excluding necessity of staying alive on the earth. A woman's confinement was a bad time for a man.

90

Creation gave her terrible strength and she got along without him. But it would pass. I saw her slim again, in black lace, starved for my arms. A first child improved their figures, ripened them. I was very happy when I got to the studio. I was reeling with love, savoring the joys to come.

My secretary was on her feet, waiting for me.

"Call your wife. It's urgent."

Even as I dialed, I saw her prostrate in the back of a taxi, a messy scene, the baby half born, Joyce moaning, the cab driver in terror, motorcycle police ripping an opening through Wilshire traffic, sirens shrieking as the cab roared to the hospital.

Joyce answered the phone.

"Your father's gone."

"Where'd he go?"

"Back to San Juan."

"But he can't. He hasn't any money."

"He's walking. Down Wilshire. I couldn't stop him."

"I'll get him."

I hung up, hurried out to the car, and raced toward Wilshire. A mile east of my house, I found him. I found him and wept. He sat on a bench on the boulevard, at a bus stop. His tool kit and roped suitcases were beside him. There on the corner he sat, an old man with his ruined possessions. He sat without hope, weary in a big town, at the edge of a river of automobiles, waves of monoxide gas flooding his tired face. Yes, I wept. I wanted to beat my breast and say, *mea culpa, mea culpa,* for I saw the pathos of the aged, the loneliness of the last years, my Papa, my old Papa, all the way from Abruzzi, a peasant to the end, sitting on the bench, alone in the world. Why, sure, I would write his story! Why, sure, we would put it down about

Uncle Mingo, for the baby to read! It was the most important thing a man had to write. I parked the car and wiped
my eyes and went to him on the bench.

"Papa. What you doing here?"

"Hello, kid."

I put my hand on his shoulder.

"What was Uncle Mingo like, Papa? Tell me the
whole thing from the beginning."

"He had red hair, kid. Big feet. Very strong man."

But he couldn't continue. He began to cry, and I cried
too, and we put our arms around one another and cried
and cried because we knew the importance of Uncle Mingo
and we loved him so much after all these years.

"Come on, Papa. Let's go home. We'll write it down.
I'm hot now, Papa. I'll write the whole damn thing."

I tried to help him from the bench, but he pulled
away.

"I got no home, kid. Nobody wants me."

"Come on, Papa. We'll get you some wine, then we'll
go home and write it."

"A little bottle, maybe."

He took out a blue polka dot bandana and wiped
his eyes and sent a blast from his nose. Then he pulled out
his pocketbook with the many compartments, and I saw
the garlic again, like a snarling little brown flame, and he
poked around and his fingers held some coins, sixty or
seventy cents, which he offered me.

"A little bottle, for your Papa."

"Put it away, Papa. I'll get you the best wine in the
world. Save your money, Papa. I got money."

We carried the luggage to the car and he got in beside
me. So he had forgiven me, and it was good to be forgiven,

and I wanted to show my thanks. We drove to a liquor store with many handsome bottles from everywhere, and he looked about, his sadness vanishing in that shimmer of beautiful bottles. Only a little wine, he insisted, something to wet his lips, maybe a pint of California wine, but the great wide world was on these shelves, and it was for my Papa. Some Cabernet from Chile, and he weakened and we ordered a few bottles; and some Château Lyonnat; and a case of golden Bordeaux, and he smiled and thought it was very foolish and expensive for a man who wanted only a sip or two of California claret. Yes, Joyce was right, and I must honor the aged, pay homage to my Papa, and he almost sobbed to hold that bottle of Chianti wrapped in straw, so we bought a case of that too.

"It's too much," he said, and he wrung his hands, but he got into the spirit of the thing presently, he lit a cigar and a shrewd merchant-prince aspect came over him, and he walked up and down the handsome store, pulling out bottles, reading labels, putting bottles back. He was a man of superb taste, he knew Portuguese brandies, and he did not forget Martell. But there was an exotic side to his nature too, for he liked the Florentine anisette made by the Italian monks, and when he saw the tall golden bottle of Galliano I knew he must have that too, an old man must have Galliano, the bottle is so exquisitely tall, the liqueur as yellow as the Italian sun.

The clerk promised quick delivery to my house, but Papa trusted only himself with the Galliano, and he felt he should bring the Martell too. We drove home and pulled into the garage. He got out carefully, measuring each movement.

Joyce was glad to see us come in together and she

kissed us, and her lips on my cheeks were the lips of a nun.

"Bless you, dearest," she said.

It was the first time in her life she ever said such a thing. Papa opened the Galliano, and the Martell, and we got comfortable in the living room. Like an alchemist in some ancient Venetian cellar, he poured himself two ounces of Martell and smiled in blissful content as he floated an ounce of Galliano upon it. He sipped, and such ecstasy seized him I thought he might float gently to the ceiling.

"My Uncle Mingo had red hair," he said. "He lived in a stone house with walls three feet thick . . ."

Joyce brought a plate of cheeses and salami.

"One time I said, 'Uncle Mingo, what makes you so strong?' Uncle Mingo, he picked me up with one hand, held me straight out, and he said, 'Olive oil.' "

We sampled the Galliano, Joyce and I.

"Uncle Mingo's brother, he was the mayor of Torcelli. We had poor roads in those days. Five thousand people. My cousin Aldo died when he was four. Everybody came to the fiesta. Cheese. Antonio didn't like the priest. Some wheat, but mostly oats. I went up there, and I said, 'Vico, what's going on here?' That was before we had electric lights . . ."

Darkness came. The phone rang many times, and Joyce tiptoed to answer it. She wouldn't let me move. I had to stay there and listen, get the facts. Papa put the Galliano aside and drank the brandy straight. The doorbell rang; some friends of Joyce. She whisked them past us quietly, to the den.

"Uncle Mingo's sister, Della, she married Giuseppe Marcosa. One day I seen d'Annunzio in town, riding a bicycle. Hot in summer, cold in winter. Big man, Uncle Mingo.

Chocolate sometimes, but no coffee. Walls, three feet thick. Maybe two acres. Plenty of rock. Six feet six, maybe. Good man. Strong. Tile roof. When Italo died, whole town was there. I said to myself, they could bring the fish from Bari, but he was no good, that Luigi. How could a man steal his own daughter's dowry? I knew there was trouble . . ."

Joyce left her guests to bring my supper on a tray. Papa wasn't hungry. I gritted my teeth and kept listening. Joyce went back to the den and her friends. Their laughter came through. Papa was half finished with the brandy.

"We didn't get no rain that year. My cousin went to Naples. Oh, we had a few grapes but the crop was poor. Olive country, rock in the soil. No barber shops in Torcelli, you cut your own. It didn't snow till the 19th of January. Uncle Mingo came over to the house, and he was mad . . ."

The doorbell rang again. It was the delivery man from the liquor store. He piled sacks and cases in the hall. Papa staggered into the kitchen and returned with a corkscrew. He opened a bottle of Chianti. For a moment I thought the ordeal was over. He swayed uncertainly, pulling at the bottle, but he came back to the living room and sat down again.

"Let me see now — where was I?"

I would see it through to the end. I would die in that room, chained to that chair, but I would hear it all. "Your Uncle Mingo came to the house, and he was mad."

"Sure he was mad! How much can a man stand? You don't know. You sit here in Los Angeles, with plenty to eat, but what do you know about a man's problems? All those rock, falling on his land. The little boy was sick. My mother went over. Wind blowing all the time. The goat died, and Dino went to Rome to be a priest. The taxes were too high.

I was seventeen before I got to Naples. Had trouble with my eyes. Uncle Mingo took off his shoe, and his foot was bleeding. We had olive oil, but the frost ruined the grape. No lights, no gas. Elena, my brother's wife, had a baby. Uncle Mingo got him by the neck, and he said, 'Alfredo, I'll break every bone in your body.' That was the night it rained. They were all afraid of Uncle Mingo . . ."

He never got to the bandits. Joyce's friends departed in respectful silence; he drank two bottles of Chianti, and he spoke of many things, but I never heard the details of Uncle Mingo and the bandits. Nearing midnight, Joyce tip-toed upstairs. We sat in the small light from a table lamp. Slowly, interminably, he went to sleep. I roused him, but still asleep he climbed the stairs, his arm around my shoulder. I helped him to his room, pulled off his clothes, and covered him up, long underwear and all.

My work was not yet finished. In the morning he would ask for the story. I went to my room and uncovered the portable. I set down the date and wrote it in the form of a letter.

> Dear Child to Be Born:
>   Tonight your Grandpa told me the story of his Uncle Mingo and the bandits. Uncle Mingo was your great-great-uncle. I write this tale because your Grandpa wishes it preserved for the day when you will be able to read and possibly enjoy it . . .

I thought it could be done in twenty minutes. But out of that chaos of jumbled anecdotes something had to emerge. It came, a mood. At four in the morning, my teeth afire from cigarettes, I was still pounding away. To hell with the kid; I could sell this one to the *Saturday Evening Post*. Through the night I heard Papa snore. I heard him rise and groan and make his way to the bathroom. There was much commotion in the hall, and the pattering of many feet. If Papa was not in possession of the bathroom, Joyce was. Out of their rooms these two people kept coming in a steady procession to the bathroom. Once I heard rapid pacing in the hall. It was Joyce, awaiting her turn. Papa emerged in his long underwear. They looked at one another, smiled in somnambulistic understanding, and went their separate ways.

I came downstairs next day at noon. I had it with me, twenty good pages about an Italian bandit, a heroic figure with red hair. I found Papa in the dining room. He had a sheet of drawing paper spread across the table, and he worked closely with a pencil and a ruler.

"Here it is, Papa. Uncle Mingo's story."

I tossed it on the drawing paper. He picked up the sheets and handed them back. "Save it for the boy."

"Don't you want to read it?"

"What I got to read it for? Good God, kid, I lived it."

FIVE

I THOUGHT it was a whim of hers, a passing fancy, but now she saw no reason to hide the facts. Since the beginning of pregnancy she had felt the pull of religion, the urgency for change. It had grown stronger with the child. At first she had concealed it, even from herself, but the deception made her miserable and she began to read, searching, the mysterious urge increasing. She had kept it from me, but during my absence up North she had made the decision: she was going to join the Church.

She was so ripe now, so juicy, so huge. The gray eyes devoured you with the child she bore, you felt yourself drowning in their hypnotic depths if you stared too long, and the passion of faith throbbed in them. I often found her staring past me, entranced in some spiritual pipe dream. At noon the Angelus sounded in the steeple of St. Boniface, the parish church. She instantly dropped whatever was at hand, her book, her comb, the dustcloth, and recited the Angelus prayers. It made me uneasy.

"Why are you embarrassed?" she asked. "You're supposed to be a liberal. Prove it, right here in your own home."

At meals she announced that we would now say grace, and I would look at Papa and he would shrug at me, and we would stare foolishly at our plates until grace was said. She was in deadly earnest. She spent hours in her room, smoking cigarettes as she lay on the bed and reflected on the fleeting quality of life. I could not fathom it. Sometimes I thought it was the fear of death in relation to childbirth. One night the old passion returned, and I slipped in beside her and put my arms around her. She was sound asleep. Then she woke, snapped on the bed lamp, got to one elbow, and stared down at me, vapors of warm piety coming from her eyes.

"You should practice self-denial," she smiled. "It will make you very strong."

"Who cares about being strong?"

"Today I read a poem. It went like this:

Take all the pleasures of all the spheres
And multiply each through endless years, —
One minute of heaven is worth them all."

I made the most dignified exit possible under the circumstances, and crawled back into my own bed, wondering where it all would end.

Twice a week she went to the rectory of St. Boniface for religious instruction. She read the catechism and a few simple tracts the priest had offered. But these were not enough. She was a rapid, voracious reader, wolfing everything she could find on the subject. She read canon law, Aquinas, à Kempis, St. Augustine, the papal encyclicals, and the *Catholic Encyclopaedia*.

One evening as I lolled in the bathtub, she knocked on the door and came in.

"Do you believe in free will?"

I could answer that one, remembering it from my schoolboy catechism.

"Certainly I believe in free will."

"Do idiots have free will? The insane?"

That wasn't in the catechism.

"I don't know about idiots."

She beamed in serenity.

"But I do."

"Hurray for you!"

In four weeks, a few days before entering the hospital, she planned to be baptized. She was having a most absorbing and difficult time selecting a patron saint. She screened them down, and out of hundreds she reduced her choice to one of two: Saint Elizabeth and Saint Anne. I did not wish to become involved in this business, but she was always talking about it.

Finally I said, "What's wrong with Saint Teresa? She's got a big reputation, all over the world."

"Too popular," Joyce said. "Not obscure, not mysterious enough. Besides, she was an awfully plain woman. Personally I lean toward Saint Elizabeth. She was very rich and very beautiful. She wrote well, too. I feel very close to Saint Elizabeth. I think she understands me better that anyone in the world."

"Isn't that just ducky."

She gave me a sweet tolerant smile.

"I'm ready for your scoffs. I've prepared myself."

"I'm not scoffing. I just don't want to become involved. I got plenty of troubles of my own."

"You're in my prayers constantly," she said. "I know how troubled you are. I was that way too, once."

"Oh, stop it."

"But I *do* pray for you. And for the baby. And for world peace."

She was suddenly irresistible, and I made a lunge for her, but all I got was a fat kiss on the cheek as the white balloon poked me in the stomach.

She went shopping for rosaries, a statue of Saint Elizabeth, and a number of crucifixes. She brought little bottles of holy water and attached a bronze font inside the door of her bedroom, within easy reach of her hand, so that she could make the sign of the cross with consecrated water whenever she entered the room. The statue of Saint Elizabeth went on an elaborate knickknack shelf in the corner. She heaped flowers before it, lit candles, and read the saint's works.

I said to Papa, "What do you think about Joyce becoming a Catholic?"

"Good. Fine."

"What's good about it?"

"Is it bad?"

"I like to plan my family."

"Then plan it. Get going. Babies."

"Babies, sure. Lots of babies. But I want them when I want them, Papa. No birth control in the Church, Papa."

"Birth control?"

"You can't stop them from coming. They just keep coming, on and on."

"Is that bad? That's good."

"We're not peasants any more, Papa. We got to stop someplace."

His eyes squinted.

"I don't like that kind of talk."

"A man should be able to say when he wants a baby."

"You heard me, kid. I don't like it."

"Suppose they come, and we got no money?"

"Get money."

"It's rough, Papa."

Up came his fist, the fingers splayed, grabbing my shirt.

"Not *my* grandchildren, understand? You leave them alone. Let them come. They got as much right here as you."

I took his fist away.

"It has nothing to do with rights, Papa. It's a question of economics."

"Cut out reading them books."

"Books—what books? I can't support too many."

"We couldn't afford none either, me and Mama. Not one. But we had four. We did it without money, a few dollars, but never enough money. You want we should use something from the drugstore, and you not even born today, without your sister and brothers, and me and Mama alone in the world? For what?"

Stated that way, it was unanswerable.

"I guess you're basically a religious man, Papa. You really believe."

"Grandchildren. That's what I believe in. And leave them books alone."

Yes, she was in deadly earnest, with the passion of a convert. She liked walking up and down before the statue of Saint Elizabeth, saying the rosary. Through the half-open door I saw her moving back and forth, she and the child, her lips reciting the beads, her eyes catching a view of herself in the mirror as she tried to pull her tummy in and up.

One morning she walked with me out to the garage.

"You know of course that we must get married as soon as possible."

"We're already married. The justice of the peace married us in Reno."

"It was a civil ceremony. As far as I'm concerned, it doesn't count."

"It counts with me."

"I want my marriage sanctified."

"You mean—we've been living in adultery all these years?"

"We'll be married after my baptism. It's a lovely ceremony. We'll be married to the end of our lives." She smiled. "You won't be able to divorce me, ever."

You do not argue with the mother of your coming child. You do the very best you can, and try to keep her happy. You have lost caste in her eyes, you are barely tolerated, the part you have played is little enough, she becomes the star of the show, and you are expected to knuckle under, for that is the way the script is written. Otherwise you might upset her, bringing anguish, and in turn upset the child.

"What do you want me to do, darling? In your own words, tell me exactly what you want me to do."

"Father Gondalfo is coming to see you. He's my instructor. I want you to talk to him."

§ § §

Two days later Father John Gondalfo came to our house. That afternoon I found him sitting in the living room with Papa and Joyce. Father Gondalfo was the hard-boiled type. He had been a Marine chaplain in the South Pacific. For over an hour he had been waiting for me. Because of the heat, he had removed his coat, and he sat in a white

T shirt, the black hair of his beefy chest seeping through the weave of the shirt. He had the arms of a wrestler and kept himself in condition by playing handball against the wall of the parish garage. He was a young priest, no more than forty-two, with a dark Sicilian face, a broken nose, and a crew haircut. He looked like a guard or tackle from Santa Clara. The moment I saw him I realized he was, like me, of Italian descent, and the consanguinity quickly established a violent familiarity. He crushed my knuckles in a handshake.

"It's five-thirty, Fante. Where you been?"

I told him, working.

"What time you knock off?"

I told him, a little past four.

"Four? Where you been, the last hour and a half?"

I told him, to Lucey's for a highball.

"Don't you know your wife's pregnant?"

Joyce sat in a big chair, the great mound lolling indolently in her lap, her knees spread slightly to support it. She adored Father John. I sensed Papa's admiration too, as well as a slight hostility toward me.

"What's wrong with drinking here in your own home?" Father John said. "With your wife and this great man who's your father? Ever think of that?"

I marveled at his shoulders, the black intensity of his eyes. "Sure, Father, I drink at home, lots."

"Time you got wise to yourself, Fante."

"Certainly, Father. But . . ."

"Don't argue with me, boy. You think I just come over on the ferry from Hoboken?"

I didn't want to argue with anybody. Looking at Joyce, I saw that she was caught up in the fervor of Father

John's vague admonition. At that moment she didn't approve of me at all. Neither did Papa, who sat before a bottle of wine, wetting his lips and nodding sagely at the priest's words.

Father John smacked his mighty hands together, rubbed them hard, and said, "Well, let's get down to business. Fante, your wife intends to join the Holy Roman Catholic Church. Any objections?"

"No objections, Father."

And that was the simple truth. There could be no objections. I might wish it otherwise, I might hope that she postpone her desire for a while, but that was something else again.

"And what about you? Your father here, this great and wonderful man, tells me that he sweated and toiled to give you a fine Catholic education. But now you read books, and, if you please, you *write* books. Just what do you have against us, Fante? You must be very brilliant indeed. Tell me all about it. I'm listening."

"I don't have anything against the Church, Father. It's just that I want to think . . ."

"Ah, so that's it! The infallibility of the Holy Father. So you want to know if the Bishop of Rome is really infallible in matters of faith and morals. Fante, I shall clear that up for you at once: he is. Now, what else is bothering you?"

I crossed to Papa, took his bottle, and swigged from it. Father John's sudden attack had me rocking on my heels, and I had to get matters quiet in my mind.

"You see, Father. The Blessed Virgin Mary . . ."

"I'll tell you about the Blessed Virgin Mary, Fante. I'll let you have it straight, without equivocation. Mary, the Mother of God, was conceived without sin, and upon her death ascended into heaven. Surely a man of your intelligence can understand that."

"Yes, Father. I will accept that for the moment. But in the mass, at the consecration . . ."

"At the consecration, the bread and wine is changed into the body and blood of Christ. What else is eating you?"

"Well, Father. When a man goes to confession . . ."

"Christ gave his priests the power to forgive sins when he said, 'Receive ye the Holy Ghost. Whose sins you shall forgive, they are forgiven them; and whose sins you shall retain, they are retained.' It's right there in the New Testament. Read it yourself."

"I understand the words, Father. But in the doctrine of original sin . . ."

"Ho! So that's it! By original sin we mean that as children of our first parents we are conceived in sin and remain so until the glorious sacrament of baptism."

"Yes, Father. I know. But the resurrection . . ."

"The resurrection? For heaven's sake, Fante, that's simple enough. Christ our Lord was crucified, and then rose from the dead, which is the promise of immortality for all of his children. Or do you choose to die like a dog, consigned forever to oblivion?"

I sighed and sat down. There was nothing more to say. Papa cleared his throat, a small smile on his lips, as he raised the bottle. There was a curious warmth to his eyes. Ash from his cigar fell in gray disorder across his lap.

"The kid reads too much, Father. I been telling him for years."

So it was "the kid" now.

"But I like to read, Papa. It's part of my trade."

"It's them books, Father. Birth control, he told me himself."

"Birth control?" Father John smiled sadly as he shook his head. "I'll tell you about birth control in the Catholic Church. There ain't any."

"I told him, Father. I said, 'I don't like that stuff.' It's not the girl's fault, Father. She's a Protestant. She don't know no better. But him: he told me. 'I like to control my family,' he told me that, coupla days ago. Me, his own father."

"I did say something like that," I admitted. "But what I meant was this, Father. My income . . ."

"You see?" Papa interrupted. "Nearly four years, they been married. Plenty time for two, a little boy and a little girl. My grandchildren. But are they here, Father? Go upstairs. Look in all the rooms, under the beds, in the closets. You won't find them. Little Nicky and little Philomena. Nicky, he'd be about three now, talking to his Grandpa. The little girl, she'd be just walking. You see them around, Father? Go out in the back yard; look in the garage. No, you won't find them, because they ain't here. And it's *his* fault!" Papa's right forefinger, the one with the broken nail, shot toward me.

"Stop it, Papa."

"I won't stop it. I want to know, because I'm their Grandpa: Where's Nicky? Where's Philomena?"

"How do I know where they are?"

Joyce went over to Papa and sat down beside him. She spoke quietly, holding his big red paw. "There haven't been any others, Papa Fante. Really and truly."

This was not the way to handle him, for he could wallow in sentimentality. Sure enough, he began to get grief-stricken, his chin jerking, his eyes suddenly wet. I tried to appeal to Joyce with my eyes. It was true that I had opposed pregnancy until we could afford it. It was also true that she had been willing to risk it without money. But I had never thought of those times as distinct human entities, or given them names, those unconceived babies, and now in Joyce's face I saw the loss, the small despair, since Papa had stated it in that sentimental fashion.

"I am talking with my blood," Papa continued. "There's two I'll never see, but they're here, someplace, and their Grandpa's not feeling so good, because he can't buy them ice cream cones."

He began to weep, poking his big knuckles into his eyes and pushing the tears away. He took another swig from the bottle and stood up, a mixture of many moods, wiping his mouth, puffing his cigar, crying, savoring the wine, pleased with his role of a despairing grandfather, yet brokenhearted because the babies were not present. Father John put an arm around him, hugging him with rough affection. They grumbled something of a farewell in Italian and Papa staggered upstairs to sleep off the wine, his chin out, his chest out, bravely up the stairs to his room, triumphantly up the stairs.

We were silent a moment. Joyce dabbed her eyes and nose with a handkerchief.

"It's the wine," I explained. "The wine makes him very sentimental."

"And you?" the priest asked.

I shrugged. "I do the best I can."

"I wonder . . ."

He had to leave us. Papa had saddened him. I helped him into his black serge coat and the three of us went outside and across the lawn to his car. We shook hands.

"Watch your language around your father," he cautioned. "He's very sensitive."

"I know."

"I want you back in the Church."

"I'll try, Father."

We watched him drive away, the car entering Wilshire Boulevard, the roar of the late afternoon traffic like a great river in the spring. We did not speak as we walked back to the house. She came into the kitchen after me, and I got out some ice cubes for a drink. In silence she watched me mix some Martinis.

"Does he help you?" I asked.

"Yes."

"He'll never be a bishop. Or even a monsignor."

"But he's really a saint. Simple, honest, never doubting."

"Simple, indeed."

"He has the faith."

"I wonder where he got his theology."

She sighed. "I admit it. Theology does give him some trouble. He can't explain the Mystical Body of Christ. And he doesn't know it, but he's really a Calvinist, and believes in predestination. All week long I've tried to straighten him out, but I can't make him understand."

Blessed be the womb that bears my son!

I kissed her and we had a Martini. She drank thoughtfully, something disturbing her. It was nearly dark now. She took her drink into the living room. In a while I went there too, looking for her in the shadowy room. She sat quietly near the window. I was surprised to find her crying softly.

"What is it, darling?"

"Your father's right about the little boy and the little girl. Oh, why didn't we have them?"

SIX

AFTER TWO WEEKS, Papa decided to begin work on the house. It was a most welcome decision. We were sick of the crude boards covering the hole in the kitchen floor. Dank and macabre smells seeped from the cracks, and everybody stumbled over the rough edges. The cleaning woman splintered her hand and refused to scrub the floor until it was repaired. Evil things came out of that hole. Every morning the first person entering the kitchen was startled by a frantic flight of clumsy brown bugs. Joyce called the Health Department and treatment was prescribed. But the DDT only staggered them, so that they rolled on their broad backs and gleefully wiggled their legs. In the night you could almost hear them down there, spraying themselves in bestial abandon.

Papa was usually the first up each morning, fixing his own breakfast but brewing enough coffee for all. He broke fast with a glass of claret in which floated a raw egg. This delicacy looked like a yellow eye pickled in vinegar. Joyce once saw him down this tidbit, and it was the first and only time she had morning sickness. Papa saved the eggshells for the coffee. They were supposed to improve the taste. We were tireless experimenters in coffee, Joyce and

I. Over the years we had tried everything, but we liked the drip method best. Each morning it was our small ritual to grind fresh coffee beans, add a pinch of salt, and pour on very hot but not boiling water. It was an unfailing method. You got what you wanted every time: good coffee.

Papa's formula was to scoop up fistfuls of ground coffee, dump them into a pot, and let them cook. Into this brew he tossed the eggshells and let it boil some more, producing a kind of coffee soup. It was ferocious coffee, eating up fresh cream with scarcely any change in color. When you stirred it up, your spoon stumbled over gravel and suspicious minutiae came to the top and sank again. Cooked egg white floated before your eyes, and you kept spitting out chips of eggshell. It was, in short, a hell of a mess. We sipped it dutifully, no more than a gesture, and I later had good coffee in my office. It was most inconvenient for Joyce. She loved coffee, and in order to get it she had to rush downstairs before Papa got there.

That morning Papa was in his working clothes. These consisted of the same things he wore on previous days, but without the necktie. There could be no doubt that he was stripped for action. His tool kit lay open on the back porch, a pencil was stuck behind his ear, and he stood before the patched hole with a mason's ruler in his hand. He seemed in deep thought, squinting at the floor through cigar smoke. We smiled gratefully. At long last the job was to be done.

It was no time to speak, each of us conscious of the importance of that moment. He had made the coffee, its burnt essence penetrating the air. Joyce got cups and saucers and set them down without a sound. Papa opened his ruler and made some obscure measurements. He removed his cigar, bit off a loose fragment, and said aloud, to himself,

"Must be two-by-tens." He closed the mason's ruler. "Got to be two-by-tens."

"You mean the joists, Papa?" I asked.

It did something to the purity of his thought. He turned slowly.

"I ever tell you how to write a story?"

"No, Papa."

"So mind your own business."

He went out to his tool kit and returned with a hammer and a short crowbar. There was a shriek of nails as he ripped off a couple of temporary boards. He lay flat on his stomach and his head disappeared inside the hole. The view proved unsatisfactory. He tore off two more boards. Now he dropped down to the ground under the house. For three or four minutes he disappeared entirely.

"He knows his business," I whispered.

"He seems very thorough."

When he emerged, cobwebs were draped about his hat and cigar, and he climbed out, spluttering and pawing his face.

"Two-by-twelves," he said. "Wonder why?"

"You mean the joists, Papa?"

He stared at me.

"You want to stay here and fix the floor, while I go and write the story?"

"I just asked, Papa."

He turned away, his eyes in a vague stare. "Two-by-tens is just as good. Just raise the piers a little. Wonder why he did it?"

"Did what, Papa?"

Without answering, he walked to the window and looked out into the driveway.

"Two-by-twelves? Hell, what's the matter with four-by-fours?"

He ducked out on the back porch and returned with a hammer. He replaced the boards over the hole and nailed them down. Gathering his tools, he dumped them into the kit. Then he disappeared into the back yard. When I went out to the garage, ready to drive to work, I found him seated under the umbrella. He rubbed his chin and seemed deeply disturbed.

"Everything okay, Papa?"

He spat a bit of cigar from his mouth.

"Go write your story, kid."

§　§　§

Early in the afternoon Joyce phoned.

"We've a surprise for you."

But I was not surprised, for I knew how this man worked. Suddenly, dramatically, he got things done.

"The best pair of hands in California," I said.

"He's a genius."

No — he was not a genius, and yet there were qualities of genius about him, a dynamic brilliance that spawned after careful cogitation. Fifty years in the building trade had made him the best man in the business. Driving home, I remembered how he had stood in the kitchen, absorbed in thought, impatient with my questions. It had worried me not a little. Was the termite damage greater than I imagined? Now it was clear that I had exaggerated the destruction. Quickly, deftly, in a burst of energy, he had finished the job, and the warmth of Joyce's voice told me she was well pleased. Once more I got that old, comfortable feeling about my

116

house and my father. Thank God he was still alive! God grant him many new years upon the earth, and God grant me the chance to show my gratitude and admiration. This was the way I felt as I drove home, locked the garage and hurried into the kitchen by way of the service porch.

The floor had not been repaired. The same rough pine boards covered the hole. Nothing had been changed. But from the front of the house I heard a pounding, the thud of steel crushing plaster. In the living room I found them, Joyce and Papa. They were tearing down the fireplace. Dust billowed from the crashing brick and plaster. They looked insane. Joyce with a hammer, Papa wielding a crowbar, attacking the brick veneer. There was a scarf around Joyce's hair, dust and dirt smeared her face. She wore green silk maternity slacks and a yellow blouse, and her face was hot and red with effort. Papa worked methodically, the cigar in his jaws, his crowbar easing brick out of the wall and dumping them to the floor. The furniture had been moved back and covered. A piece of canvas protected the floor.

Then Joyce saw me.

"Hello," she cried.

"What's going on around here?"

"We're building a new fireplace."

"What for?"

I stared at the wreckage. The old fireplace, for all its simplicity, had been adequate. I had tested it once and it had burned well, without smoke. It had not been a work of art but it suited the living room.

"There's nothing wrong with that fireplace."

Joyce brushed the dust from her clothes. "I've always hated it. From the day I laid eyes on it."

"But you should have talked to me first."

"Why? It *had* to be done."

"It didn't *had* to be done."

"It's got to come down," Papa said.

"What's wrong with it?"

He nodded at Joyce's dust-covered bump. "Ask my grandson there. He don't want no Los Angeles fireplace. He wants a fireplace his Grandpa built."

Chattering with excitement, Joyce showed me the plans Papa had drawn on a long sheet of foolscap. It was to be a massive hearth, six feet high and ten feet broad, constructed of thin strips of Arizona flagstone. Black mortar would fill the joints. A thick unbroken stone would form the mantelpiece. According to the specifications, it was exactly twice the size of the fireplace they were demolishing. It was truly magnificent. It belonged in a Swiss chalet, a hunting lodge, or an Elks' Club.

"But you'll have to tear out part of the wall too," I said.

"You leave that to me," Papa said.

Joyce's arms went out to it.

"It's going to be lovely. So big and handsome. We'll be so warm and cozy."

"Great," I said. "Specially when the temperature drops to twenty-five below zero, and eighteen feet of snow paralyzes the traffic on Wilshire Boulevard."

"For my grandson," Papa said dreamily. "It'll last a thousand years. Nothing in the world's gonna knock down that fireplace. Last longer than anything in Los Angeles."

I pictured the scene, not a thousand years hence, but only ten or fifteen, when our house would doubtless be torn down to make room for a parking lot, cars driving in and out, but always around Papa's indestructible fireplace, because it defied all efforts to tear it down.

"Papa," I said. "When you gonna fix that hole in the kitchen floor?"

"That's no job for me. Get a carpenter."

§ § §

I was opposed to this thing. There was a kind of insanity about it. There followed worrisome days. The materials arrived. They were dumped on the front lawn. four tons of flagstone, a mountain of sand, a pile of brick, sacks of cement, pieces of lumber. Troubled days, big holes in my house, a pregnant wife who now fancied herself a hod carrier, and an old man with a passion for building.

It was the mortar that fascinated her. Papa built a box in which to mix it: lime, cement, sand and black coloring. She could not resist the stuff. She bought canvas gloves and a wide-brimmed Mexican hat. All day long she prodded the mortar with a hoe, kneading it, stroking it, adding water. She was like a child making mud pies. It splattered her shoes, soiled her slacks. A pregnant woman should not mix mortar. You will not find it recommended in any of the books. I cautioned her against overdoing it. She scoffed. She denied it. But the stuff left telltale black spots on her sandals, on her elbows, in her hair. Even with the canvas gloves she developed a blister on her thumb.

"I burned it at the stove," she lied.

Papa did the heavy work. He mixed the mortar, carried it to the fireplace in buckets, dumped it on the mortar board. He cut the stones, piled them into a wheelbarrow and trucked them to the fireplace. He handled the brick. But she was always fooling around. Certain stones she liked;

119

big or small, she carried them to the job. They were pretty stones, she said, and she wanted them to show. But they were heavy, and she pulled them, dragged them, tried to lift them. Then back to the mortar.

"Give it a little water, Miss Joyce."

She gave it a little water, then she hoed it, smoothed it. Or she sat and watched him work, and he asked for things.

"Hammer."

"Level."

"Trowel."

One day at noon I caught her red-handed in the front yard, shoveling sand into the mortar box. She could not deny it because she wasn't ten feet in front of me, the shovel in her hands, drops of perspiration clinging to her temples. I took the shovel away from her.

"Stop behaving like a fool."

She tossed her chin and sailed into the house. I went after her. She stood at the fireplace, her arms folded, her eyes guilty and away from me.

"Keep this up and you'll have a miscarriage."

"Who's miscarriage?" Papa said.

"I don't want her lifting things, shoveling things."

"Won't hurt her."

"I'm not taking any chances."

"Won't hurt her. Back in Abruzzi, woman works right up to the last day, washing clothes, cleaning house, fixing the land. Good for mother. Keeps the muscles strong."

She turned to him.

"All it needed was a little sand, Papa. Just a shovel or two."

"Shovel or two won't hurt nothing." He glanced

at her, his eyes going soft and pleased.

"Nice little boy. Grandpa's boy."

"Look, Papa. She's my wife. She'll ruin her health. This isn't Italy. She's not used to it."

"And he's my grandson. And he's going to be fine."

§ § §

They were ranged against me, and a wall separated us, a fireplace. I went to see her in the quiet of the night, tiptoeing past the room out of which Papa's snores came like a bomb whistle. She was glassy-eyed from canon law, startled at my presence, and back to her book again.

"How do you feel?"

"Fine."

"It won't be long now."

Silence.

"I don't care any more," I said. "Boy or girl, it suits me fine."

Silence.

"You've got to be very careful from now on."

She put the book aside, took off her reading glasses and stared at me oddly.

"If I should die, you won't be able to marry my sister."

"I don't want to marry your sister."

"She's very attractive. But you'll never be able to have her. Never. It's the law of the Church."

"But I'm not interested in your sister."

"It wouldn't do you any good, even if you were."

"But I'm not."

"It's a very good law. A very wise law."

"What makes you think you're going to die?"

"I'm not going to die. I said, *if* I should die."

Ominous words. Was there some premonition of tragedy within the depths of her? What stirrings in the secret places of her psyche prompted her to become fascinated by this phase of Church law? Carefully I considered the situation. My thought was of Dr. Stanley. If we had not pestered him so much in the past, I would have called him. Alas, too often had we cried wolf. If among my friends there was one mother who could talk to this foolish girl about the folly of lifting things. But I knew no mothers. I knew plenty of wives, but no mothers.

The days of shameful trickery. For I tried to catch her now. Coming home from the office, I drove into the alley from the north instead of the south, hoping to surprise her at the mortar box. Once I parked a block away and walked the remaining distance. That time she was not in the front yard.

Thus it was that I caught her again. That afternoon I quit work at two, drove to within a block of my house, and parked around the corner. I walked the rest of the way. From that distance I surprised her. She was on her knees beside the pile of stones, her two small hands gripping a short-handled sledge. She was pounding a piece of flagstone, breaking it into smaller segments for the fireplace. With a shout I rushed toward her. She dropped the sledge, suppressed a cry, and ran into the house. I jumped the fence and went right after her. She was not in the living room. Papa was at the fireplace, a trowel in his hand.

"Where's my wife?"

He shrugged innocently.

I climbed the stairs. She had locked herself in the

bathroom. I could hear the hiss of water in the shower. I went into her bedroom. Everything was in readiness for the most important event of her life. A week ago she had packed a grip for her stay in the hospital.

It lay open on the stand, and I looked through it. Combs, a brush, a hand mirror. A clock. Bedroom slippers. A box of stationery. A fountain pen. Gowns. A dressing robe. A manicure set. Cologne. A few handkerchiefs, a few pins. The many small things in a woman's life. Piled in the corner were the gifts she had received at a baby shower: toys, bottles, blankets, baby clothes, a little silver dish, a tiny fork and spoon. Off her bedroom was the glassed-in porch she planned for a nursery. Here was the crib, a chiffonier, a bassinet, a rocking horse, a doll. Pink was the motif, pink for girls, pink curtains, pink ribbons.

So let it be a girl. But boy or girl, give it a chance, let it live! It was time for a showdown. The bathroom door opened and she came into the room. She looked at me without surprise. The shower had washed the make-up from her face, her lips were a faded red, and her wet hair hung like a rag mop.

"Well?" she said.

"I want to talk to you."

"Really?"

She began to brush her hair.

"I want you to stop fooling around. No more lifting. No more breaking stones."

"Is that all?"

I wanted to shake her.

"I've come to a decision. Stop it, or I leave this house."

She smiled and tossed her wet hair.

"You can leave any time."

"Is that your decision?"

"Yes, darling."

Grimly I walked out. The choice was hers. She alone had made it. But I didn't leave. You can't leave them when they are in that condition. It requires great tact. Nor should you make rash statements. It requires great forbearance, but you can't leave.

SEVEN

RETRIBUTION was inevitable. Two nights later she paid for her folly. It was ten minutes after midnight when she entered my room. One glance at the chalky face, the wide eyes, and I knew her time was at hand. Dr. Stanley had predicted first labor around the 25th. This was the 12th. But Dr. Stanley had not anticipated a siege of mixing mortar and crushing stones.

Leaning in the doorway, one hand on the bump, the other against her forehead, she said, "I think the baby's coming."

I jumped out of bed. She gritted her teeth as cramps seized her and she studied her wrist watch, breathing hard.

"Nine minutes. They're getting worse."

I led her to the bed. There was sweat at her temples and she trembled. Her hand in mine was hot, wet and shaking. Together we stared at the wrist watch. Ten minutes later she had another seizure. It lasted thirty seconds. She took it with gritted teeth, clenched fists. I remembered warnings from the books.

"How about the bag of waters?"

"Call Dr. Stanley. Get me to the hospital."

I ran downstairs and telephoned the doctor. A nurse

JOHN FANTE

answered. She would deliver my message; the doctor would call back. Upstairs Joyce lay stretched full length on the bed. I called Papa.

"The baby's coming."

He wakened instantly.

"Where?" He sat up. "The baby?" He was out of bed. "How?"

He staggered out of the darkness in his long underwear. Joyce moaned. Papa pulled on his overalls. I went back to the bedroom. Joyce lay with eyes closed.

"How about the bag of waters?"

"Give me a cigarette."

Buckling his overall straps, Papa entered. In a glance he appraised the situation.

"You. Go downstairs and boil some water."

"What for?"

"Do what I tell you."

I couldn't move. All my life in such situations I knew they boiled water. What did they do with it?

"We've got to get her to the hospital."

"God damn it, boil some water."

He got me by the nape of the neck and shoved me through the door. All the way downstairs I knew it was madness. The hospital was only ten minutes away. I filled the teakettle with water, put it over the gas flame and hurried upstairs. Papa sat on the bed beside Joyce, holding her hand.

"Did you call Dr. Stanley?"

"His nurse is getting him."

"Call Father Gondalfo. I want to be baptized."

"Hot water," Papa said.

The phone rang. I rushed downstairs. It was the voice of Dr. Stanley.

126

"The baby's coming, Doc."

"It seems a bit early. Is she in labor?"

"She's in agony."

"Are the pains regular? Did she time them?"

"Every ten minutes. She's in agony."

"You'd better bring her down."

"Okay, Doc."

I went upstairs.

"Get ready, honey. We're going to the hospital."

"Hot water," Papa yelled.

"Call Father Gondalfo," Joyce moaned. "I want to be baptized."

The kettle downstairs began to whistle, then shriek as the water came to a boil. I called Father Gondalfo. He promised to be at the hospital in fifteen minutes. I grabbed the kettle of hot water and carried it upstairs. Joyce was in her room, seated on the bed, a fur coat around her, bedroom slippers on her feet. Papa tore the kettle out of my hands.

"Get the car. Bring it around front."

He rushed the kettle into the bathroom. I followed him. I wanted to see this.

"Get going," he said. "The car."

I just stood there. I didn't want him using any of his Abruzzian techniques on Joyce. He took a bottle of brandy from the medicine cabinet and poured a big slug of it into a water tumbler. Then he added hot water and held the mixture up to the light.

"What're you up to?"

"What do you suppose?"

He put away the drink in one breathless gulp. It burned all the way down.

"Ha-a-a!" he said. "Now I feel better. Get going, you."

I rushed downstairs, backed the car out of the garage, and drove it around front. They were waiting for me at the curb. The three of us sat up front. Papa put his arm around Joyce's shoulder. She was not in pain.

All the way to the hospital there were no seizures. None of this felt like impending fatherhood, and I had the murky feeling that the whole thing was a false alarm. It felt like hysteria rather than fatherhood; it seemed shapeless, smoky, like an unexplained explosion. I went along with it because I couldn't be sure. There was caution in Joyce's face now; there was restraint and worry. Papa had an unlit cigar in his mouth.

"Everything's gonna be fine," he said.

The statement had no texture, no honesty. The nearer the hospital, the greater our unspoken certainty that the whole thing was badly miscalculated.

Then I said it. I had to say it: "Maybe it really isn't your time yet, darling."

It brought a howl of dismay from Joyce.

"Oh, please!" she cried. "Don't even *think* it! I'll die if you do."

With his left hand Papa reached over and yanked my hair.

"Leave her alone, you damn fool."

"It's just a thought I had."

"Then cut it out. After all *you* done!"

"Me? I didn't do anything."

At first I didn't realize his meaning. I looked at him, his eyes sharp and popping with anger. It was a chute into his mind. Then I knew. He was still thinking of the time I sold his concrete mixer to buy a bicycle. It had happened nearly twenty years ago, but there it was, the old bitterness, flaring up at this odd time.

"Please, Papa. Not *that* again."

The cigar trembled with his chin. The old bitterness had rendered him speechless.

Joyce began to sob.

"I'm so miserable."

His arm tightened around her shoulder.

"After the baby, you come and live with Mama and me," he soothed. "Get away from this fellow. He brings nothing but trouble. I shoulda sent him to reform school."

I clung tightly to the wheel and kept still. We entered the circular driveway before the main gate of the hospital. On the front steps loomed the big figure of Father Gondalfo. He opened the door as I stopped the car.

"Oh, Father!" Joyce sobbed.

Papa got out. The two men helped Joyce step down. Her eyes were wet from crying. The priest laid his large hands on her shoulders and comforted her.

She wept softly. Now Papa and Father Gondalfo began an exchange of crackling Italian. They waved their arms, shook their heads, frowned, grunted, sneered, smiled, groaned, rolled their eyes, grimaced, swayed, pointed at me, and finally lapsed into brooding silence, looking at one another in unhappy bewilderment. Then the giant priest poked his head inside the car door and looked at me, his dark eyes eating me up.

"You, there. Park the car."

Why not? At a time like this, it was a father's solemn duty to park his car. I drove across the street to the vast hospital parking area. When I walked back to the hospital entrance, they were gone. I entered the reception room.

They had taken the elevator and were already somewhere upstairs. I asked the nurse at the desk where they had gone. She wouldn't tell me. I had to sign some papers before she would talk about it. Then she told me to see the nurse on the twelfth floor.

It was bad up there too. I couldn't learn anything. Papa and Father Gondalfo were out of sight. The chief nurse informed me that Joyce was being examined by Dr. Stanley. She was a short, thick-chested woman with a red face and rippling muscles in her arms. She was too busy to talk to me. Her desk was covered with papers and ledgers.

"What room is she in?" I asked.

"You can't see her anyway."

"But I'm her husband."

"I thought the old man was her husband."

"He's my mother's husband. He's my father."

She returned to her papers. Other nurses came and went. I stood there, trying to keep out of the way. The phone kept ringing. An interne informed the chief nurse that 1231 wanted orange juice. She sneered and said, "No orange juice." Above her, on the opposite wall, was an electric box with a glass face. A number kept appearing and disappearing in the glass. Number 1214, a red number. It came and went with frantic urgency. Nobody paid any attention to it, neither nurses nor internes.

"Is my wife in 1214?"

"No."

I nodded at the glass.

"Somebody in 1214 wants something."

"Young man, please go to 1245 and sit down."

I went everywhere, looking for 1245. I walked up one hall and down another. I couldn't find it. The room numbers would be in sequence, and then there would be a series of unnumbered doors. I tried a door without a number and a woman sat up in bed and said, "Get out of here." I finally found my way back to the chief nurse.

"I can't seem to find 1245."

She was convinced of my vast stupidity, for 1245 was right there, next to her desk. She didn't even speak to me, she only looked at the door and let her eyes roll back to me. I thanked her, but there was no hiding her low opinion of me.

Papa and Father Gondalfo sat in 1245. They froze as I entered. Papa turned his back on me. Father Gondalfo waited for me to sit down in one of the leather chairs.

"A man and his wife have many problems," he began. "Sometimes they seem too much to bear. They lose their tempers. It's only human to lose your temper."

"Where is she?" I interrupted. "What did they do with her?"

"Now he wants to know," Papa sneered. "After all he's done."

Father Gondalfo raised his hand for peace. Papa ignored it.

"I seen this kid chase her upstairs. She had to lock herself in the water closet. That's when it happened, running up the stairs."

"Let's not jump to conclusions," the priest said. "Let's wait until we hear what the doctor has to say."

"I hope nothing's wrong with my grandson," Papa said. "I'll kill him if anything happened."

I was sick of him.

"Oh, shut up, Papa."

He stared beseechingly at the priest. At last he was

vindicated. At last I had demonstrated my worthlessness. His overalls and broken-down shoes didn't help matters either.

Then Joyce entered with Dr. Stanley. She was calm, chastened, and seemed more pregnant than ever.

"Wrap her up and take her home," the doctor smiled.

"Everything all right?" Papa asked.

"Fine, fine. Come back in a week or so."

"I'm so ashamed," Joyce said.

"It happens all the time. Forget it."

"No action from the bag of waters," I said. "That was the tip-off."

"You and your bag of waters," Joyce said.

She was changed, chastened. It was mostly embarrassment. She wanted to be out of there. The doctor followed us as we trooped to the elevators. She hugged the fur around her, hiding her face. There was very little to say. We were leaving the place without a baby, empty-handed. The big priest towered over us. In complete silence we waited for the elevator. Papa looked like a tramp. I got behind a post, out of sight of the cynical nurses. I shared Joyce's embarrassment. We seemed forever to be coming and going from this hospital. We were always harassing this doctor. We had probably got him out of a sound sleep. He had not delivered a baby. Now we were going home. The procedure seemed endless, stretching into eternity. Next week we would do it all over again.

The elevator arrived and we stepped in: a pregnant woman, her husband, her father-in-law, and her spiritual adviser. With the old man who operated the elevator there were five of us. It was a massive elevator, it was like a ballroom. Thirty people could easily have ridden in it without crowding. But standing there, saying good-by once more to the smiling doctor, there was scarcely room to breathe. The mound under the fur coat seemed to fill the whole elevator. Crammed together, crushed in a thick human mass, we descended in grim silence. Only when we got to the main floor did a sense of freedom return.

Then Joyce said, "I forgot my grip."

They all looked at me.

Why not? Who else?

I took the elevator back to the twelfth floor. The grip was beside the chief nurse's desk. I picked it up.

"Just a minute."

"It's my wife's. She's not staying. She forgot it."

"What's your name?"

I told her.

"That's the old man's name."

"He's my father."

"You're the husband?"

"Right."

Silence.

"May I take the grip?"

"It's yours, isn't it?"

I rode down to the main floor. They were waiting for me on the steps outside.

"Get the car," Papa said.

I got the car. Papa and Joyce settled in the front seat. Father Gondalfo had come in the parish car. We thanked him for his trouble.

"It's God's will," he said to Joyce. "And it's for the best. Now you'll have time to complete your instructions."

We said good-by. He walked toward the parking lot, the gravel snarling under his feet. I drove away. Joyce sat quietly, full of sadness and new wisdom. I leaned over and kissed her.

"How do you feel?"

"Very tired. And very foolish."

A big sigh came from Papa.

"It takes a long time to make a son."

EIGHT

PEACE IN my house, quiet, a time of great calm. She became another woman again. She was out of the fable now, out of the novels, a tale of motherhood, a woman in waiting. No more breaking of stones or mixing mortar. I never saw her so beautiful. She walked on quiet feet, a different perfume trailing after her. Every morning she went to early Mass. Every afternoon she visited the parish house for instructions. Father Gondalfo was rushing it a little, but it was at her insistence. In the evenings I walked with her to the church. She said the rosary, made the stations of the cross, or simply sat quietly, her hands folded in her lap.

It was a strange time for me. I sat beside her, not able to pray, to articulate a feeling for Christ. But it all came back to me, the memory of the old days when I was a boy and this cool and melancholy place meant so much. From the beginning she had assumed I would return with her. It had seemed the right thing to do. Somehow I would capture the old feeling, the reaching out with the fingers of my soul and grasping the rich fine joy of belief. Somehow I had felt it was always there, that I had but to move toward it with only a murmur of desire and it would cloak me in the vast comfort of God's womb. There was the scent of incense, the creaking of pews, the play of sunlight through stained-glass windows, the cool touch of holy water, the laughter of little candles, the stupendous reaching back into antiquity, the baffling realization that countless millions before me had been here and gone, that other billions would come and go through a million tomorrows. These were my thoughts as I sat beside my wife. These and the gradual realization that I had been wrong, that it was not easy to come back to your church, that the Church changeless was always there, but that I had changed. The drift of years had covered me like a mountain of sand. It was not easy to emerge. It was not easy to call out with a small voice and feel that I was being heard. I sat beside her, and I knew it would be very hard. Nay, I knew it would be almost impossible.

I sat beside her and enjoyed the sensation of a new kind of thinking. For one's thoughts were different here. Outside, beyond the heavy oak doors, you thought of taxes and insurance, of fade-outs and dissolves, you weighed the matter of Manhattans and Martinis, you suspected your agent of treachery, your friend of disloyalty, your neighbor of stupidity. And yet I could sit beside her before the altar, her small hands exquisite in green kid gloves, and I could adore her for the beauty of her effort, the striving of her heart, the mighty force that prompted her to be but a good woman, humble and grateful before God. I could sit beside her, my own lips dry for lack of words, I, the phrasemaker, and the pages of my soul were blank and unlettered, and I turned them one after another, seeking a rhyme, a few scattered words to articulate the fact that in this place I thought not of taxes and insurance, and my agent, my neighbor and friend were somehow disembodied, they assumed a spirituality, a beauty; they were entities and not beings, they were souls and not swine.

Yet, in spite of it all, I was not ready. Born a Catholic, I could not bring myself to return. Perhaps I expected too much; a shudder of joyful recognition, the dazzling splendor of faith reborn. Whatever it was, I could not return. There before me was the road, the signposts clearly marking the direction to peace of soul. I could not take the road. I could not believe that it was so easy. I was sure that beyond the next hill lay trouble.

§ § §

Four days before the baby was born, Joyce entered the Church. She was christened Joyce Elizabeth. The ceremony took place in the evening at the baptismal font in the Church of St. Boniface. Her sponsor in baptism was our neighbor from across the street, Mrs. Sandoval. She was a tall serene woman in her sixties. Father Gondalfo had selected her because she lived near us, and because we knew no Catholics in town.

Joyce's happiness was almost terrifying. As Father Gondalfo read the ritual, first in Latin, then in English, the tears ran freely down her cheeks and crashed on her bump. Hers was a shattering kind of happiness. She was almost grief-stricken with it. I stood with my father in the background, watching, listening to her sobs as they echoed through the empty church like the flapping of wings.

All of us were badly shaken. Papa dabbed his cheeks with a large blue bandanna. Mrs. Sandoval smiled bravely, unashamed of her tears. The ceremony was long, for the priest gave her absolute baptism. This cleansed her not only of original sin, but of all the sins of her life. She wept steadily, until Father Gondalfo became choked up too, his eyes blinded as he broke off the ceremony to dig a handkerchief from under his cassock and wipe his eyes.

"We shouldn't cry," he whispered. "This is a time for happiness."

It provoked a fresh outburst from Joyce. Papa and I led her to one of the pews, where she knelt heavily, her face a smear of make-up, mascara and tears.

"I'm sorry," she wept. "I'm terribly sorry, but I can't help it. I'm so happy."

"Your face is a mess," I said.

She stopped crying instantly. She opened her compact and fixed her face. Without a word she returned to the baptismal font and the ceremony continued. Quietly, her eyes cast down, her hands folded, she experienced the purification of her soul. Then it was over. It was over for Joyce, but not for me.

Afterward, we gathered outside the church. Mrs. Sandoval had a baptismal gift for Joyce—a silver Saint Christopher's medal. Joyce was delighted with her godmother. They walked arm in arm to Mrs. Sandoval's car. We waved good-by as the older woman drove away.

The moment I had dreaded now arrived. I looked at my wife. There were stars in her hair, stars in her eyes that, bathed in tears a moment ago, shone now with high happiness. It seemed absurd that her conversion should make a great difference, and yet it was so. She was not the old Joyce. She was not the Joyce of even an hour ago. There was no solving the chemistry of this change, I only felt it, knew it, saw it. The thing I felt was a maturity, a quality of womanhood not associated with her pregnancy; a tradition, rather an identification with Mother Church, with the Church's high reverence for women, an elevation of her to that state I felt for the Virgin Mary as a boy. We looked at one another, and in that moment she too knew that I had sensed the change, the all-pervading transformation of her personality. We looked at one another, and in that moment each of us knew that this night was a milestone in our lives, and that our lives together were terribly important, terribly serious. But it was a sad moment too, because I cherished the nonsense of living, the trivia, the fooling around, and that we had put behind us.

The big hand of Father Gondalfo, the heavy arm, came down around my shoulder. "Well, you ready?"

He meant: Was I ready to go to confession?

I wanted to say: No, Father.

I said: "Yes, Father."

"Good. Tomorrow you can receive holy communion together. The Mass will be for you. Afterward, I'll marry you at the main altar."

"That's fine, Father."

We walked back into the church. The priest genuflected and went down the side aisle to one of the three confession booths. Heavy purple curtains draped each entrance. Father Gondalfo disappeared inside the center booth. He turned on a light. Joyce, Papa and I walked down the center aisle and entered a pew directly across from the confessional.

I knelt down to examine my conscience. After fifteen years, I was going to confession again. What were the sins I had committed in a decade and one half? The task before me was enormous. It was so vast that I could not take it seriously. Worse, I felt no contrition. I regretted nothing.

Good and evil, I had enjoyed it all. The laying on of the priest's hands in absolution seemed meaningless. I could not, I would not enter the confessional. In the old days my very blood sang in answer to the call of absolution. Gladly I used to fall on my knees and pour out my troubles and become cleansed and walk away with the mighty muscles of a pure heart. I clutched at the past. I found nothing.

Time passed, fifteen minutes, a half hour, with the priest waiting patiently. The tussle with my conscience left me exhausted. How could I confess that for which I had no remorse? Wearily I sat down beside Papa and Joyce.

"I can't do it," I whispered.

Papa looked startled.

"Please try," Joyce smiled.

"I can't. It's hypocrisy."

Papa consulted hurriedly with Joyce.

"What's wrong with him?"

"He doesn't want to go," Joyce whispered.

"He's *got* to go." His voice was loud.

I shook my head.

"Can't, Papa."

"Get in there!"

"I tell you I can't."

"You been a bad boy. Go in, get in there!"

He grabbed me by the nape of the neck and tried to push me toward the confessional. I clung to the pew and refused to budge. His face reddened with effort. Suddenly he was on his feet and moving quickly toward the confessional. We watched him in surprise. He turned to look back at us, his eyes desperate. Then he entered the confession booth.

I learned later that it was his first confession in fifty-five years. He never explained why he had done it. I was certain he had not planned to go, had never dreamed of going. But in his own fashion he had done this thing for me, for his grandchild, because it had to be done.

His confession was in the nature of an argument. It was given in Italian — a rumbling discussion, indistinct and intense. Whenever Father Gondalfo said anything, Papa answered sharply. The priest in turn raised his voice. They talked with their hands too, for you could see the curtains flapping. Finally the confessor's voice prevailed. No word came from Papa. The priest spoke gently, persuasively, a soothing whisper. When they emerged, both men were tired and perspiring. Papa dropped on his knees in the nearest pew. Father Gondalfo smiled and patted him on the shoulder. Papa covered his face with two hands, crushing out all distraction as he said his penance. The priest shot me a disheartening glance. I got up and walked outside. He was waiting for me on the steps.

"What happened?"

"I couldn't make it."

"Would you like another confessor? I could call Father Shaw. Would that help?"

"I don't think so."

"I'm bitterly disappointed. You know, of course, what this means?"

I knew: It meant that I was not in the state of grace. It meant I could not go to communion with Joyce the next morning. It meant that I could not receive the sacraments, and marriage was a sacrament.

"I'm sorry, Father. I'll keep trying."

He turned to Joyce and Papa as they came out of the church. We said good night. Papa refused to look at me.

141

We walked to the car. I took Joyce's hand.

"You're disgusted with me."

"I'm disappointed, of course."

"Give me a little time. I'll do it some day."

"That's what I can't understand. If you're coming back to the Church some day, why not now?"

"I don't know."

"I don't either."

"I'm gonna take a little walk," Papa said.

We watched him move toward the corner. He had a quick bouncy step. He paused under the street lamp to light a cigar. The smoke drifted back toward us, fragrant in the night air. We didn't speak as we drove home. I locked the garage and we walked into the house. In silence we went upstairs. I hesitated before my door, hoping she would speak. She entered her room without turning around. I pulled off my coat and threw myself on the bed. I could feel no grief for what I had done, no remorse. It exasperated me that there was not so much as a quiver of regret. It left me lacerated and miserable.

Then she came through the door, the white balloon floating under her nightgown, a book in her hand. Smiling, she looked down at me.

"I want to read something," she said.

And she read: "O father, O mother, O wife, O brother, O friend, I have lived with you after appearances hitherto. Henceforward I am the truth's. Be it known unto you that henceforward I obey no law less than the eternal law. . . . I appeal to your customs. I must be myself. I cannot break myself any longer for you or you. If you can love me for what I am, we shall be the happier. If you cannot I will seek to deserve that you should.

I will not hide my tastes or aversions."
 "Emerson," I said. "Oh, sweet man!"
 She bent down and kissed me.
 "Good night," she whispered.
 Blessed be the womb that bears my son!
 I cried with happiness.

NINE

WE WERE playing chess the night it happened. We had been expecting it at any moment, our lives had stopped still to wait for the coming of the child, and this was the night. Papa had finished the fireplace. He had rushed the work, for it was most important to have it completed and ready for the new Fante, like a gift wrapped and tied with pink bows. The very house breathed with anticipation. The new one was coming, and a kind of loneliness held us because he was not already there. The hard work of that day had tired Papa and he had gone to bed.

"Call me if anything happens," he had said.

At ten o'clock we sat at the chessboard, and it was my move.

"Your queen is in danger," she said.

I interposed a bishop and the queen was safe. Now it was her move. She was a fast player, but she made no move for a long time; too long, it seemed, and I looked up from the board to her face, wondering what delayed her.

"Your move."

She was not listening, only staring into my eyes, her face flushed, her breathing hard, until her cheeks became very red, and I saw that she was intent on some curious activity inside her.

"Something popped," she whispered.

"Popped? What popped? I didn't hear anything."

"I don't know. But I distinctly heard a pop."

We listened. She covered her mouth.

"Oh, dear. It's the bag of waters."

"Let's go to the hospital."

She hesitated before rising.

"Please," she smiled. "Don't look. Hide your eyes."

I covered my eyes as she stood up and started across the room. I heard her scampering up the stairs, breathless, saying, "Oh, dear," and "Dear me," and "Oh, my goodness." When I knew she was out of sight I called the doctor. Upstairs I heard Joyce in the bedroom, her heels clicking on the floor. I ran up there. She was sitting on the bed, reading a book called *The Coming Child.*

"We ought to get started. I called the doctor."

"I want to be sure this time. Absolutely sure."

"It's real. I know it's real."

"Listen." She read: "At the beginning of labor, the pain generally begins in the small of the back. It begins in the manner of a slight pinch or backache, rising in crescendo fashion until it reaches a peak of intensity which persists for several seconds, and then it gradually diminishes . . ."

The very thing she read happened at that precise moment. The book fell from her hands and she sat perfectly still, looking down at the bump. Her hands moved to touch it, feel it.

"Contracting uterus," she said. "Page 158. Read it."

I got the book off the floor, but I had too many

hands, too many fingers. I couldn't even hold the book. It fell to the floor. The pain sharpened, then eased off. She whistled softly.

"I'm ready to go now."

This time it was easy. We had rehearsed the whole thing before. Quietly we stepped into the hall, listening to Papa's whistling snores, and then down the stairs. Without saying it, we both understood that it was best not to waken Papa. Under the mock orange tree in the back yard she stopped and put her arms around me.

"You've been wonderful," she said. "I'll never complain again."

"Let's get going, honey."

"There's time. I want you to know that I've behaved very badly for nine months. I've been a complete idiot. Really, it's nothing to have a baby. It's very easy."

"You haven't had it, dear. Let's go."

I pulled her toward the garage. She got into the car and sat far away from me, against the opposite door. She fumbled through her purse for a pack of cigarettes, offering me one too.

"Shall I light it for you?" she asked.

"Please."

"Some men prefer to light their own."

It seemed a curious remark, but I didn't answer. We drove leisurely, for we were old hands at this business. There was really no hurry. The night was warm and you could smell the big white magnolias along Normandie. At a boulevard stop she had more pain. It was worse. I watched her grab the door latch and hang on.

"Rough," I said.

Sweat stood out on her forehead. Her eyes rolled

147

with the pain. Her great paunch seemed to crush her into the corner. It was like a big hive of bees, seething with the dimensions of pain. When the seizure subsided she gave a faint whistle of relief.

"It's nothing," she said. "Of course, it hurts a little, but it's nothing like what my mother said."

"We'll be there in five minutes."

"I'm so glad. Then you'll be rid of me. I hate burdening you with all this."

"It's not a burden."

"All my life I've been a burden. It's the fate of women. We're not very nice, really, we're not."

"You're talking nonsense."

"It isn't nonsense. Look at me, I'm a cow, that's what I am. Grotesque and uninteresting. Nobody could possibly love me. And you mustn't ever tell me you love me again. Because I know you can't. And I don't deserve your love. How good you've been! How patient! I'm terribly grateful. Forgive me for everything."

She began to cry, her tight bloated face too round to gather the tears that slid into her lap. Another pain took hold of her, and her teeth came together and her fists tightened until it subsided.

"I'm not very brave," she panted. "But I don't want to be brave. I just want to crawl into some hole somewhere, out of your sight, and suffer and suffer, because I don't deserve you. I'm glad I'm suffering. I've been a fool. I deserve it."

She made me very unhappy. She sat with her legs spread apart, her pouch bouncing, her face like a tear-stained basketball, and for a moment I forgot that it was only a temporary thing, and the theme of her misery got hold of me too, and I began to think I was indeed a most unfortunate man to ever have attached myself forever to this quivering mass of gurgling flesh. I drove along with wet eyes, weeping for myself, fascinated by my courage and undiminished loyalty. How right she was! How noble, how long-suffering I had been. It was fated that she should suffer, it was good that she should experience pain, to atone for the frightful manner she had treated me through her pregnancy. And how perceptive she was now that her day of atonement had arrived! How attenuated the delicate balance of her sense of morality. Thank God she at last saw the wickedness of her ways!

When we reached the hospital, I followed the curving driveway that led to a stone canopy where ambulances disembarked their patients. She stayed in the car while I went inside. At the reception desk I filled out papers freeing the hospital of all responsibility for whatever might happen to my wife, and while this was going on the woman in charge telephoned for nurses and a wheel chair. By the time I got back to the car, two nurses had already helped Joyce into a wheel chair and wrapped blankets around her. I watched them wheel her into the elevator. Then I parked the car and came back to the hospital with Joyce's suitcase. I got into the elevator and rode to the twelfth floor.

By now I was very familiar with the twelfth floor. I almost swaggered in easy recognition as the elevator doors slid open and I stepped out. Far down the clean rubber-carpeted hall I saw the two nurses wheel my wife through a door. Joyce tossed her head back and caught a glimpse of me coming forward. The wheel chair stopped and the nurses paused in the doorway. They swung the wheel chair around so that Joyce faced me. She held out her arms, smiling.

I swallowed back my sudden joy. How could there be so much beauty in all the world? Those hands of hers, out to me, those gentle fingers, out to me; her eyes, out to me; her mouth, her lips, out to me, pouring love and mysterious heartbreaking beauty out to me, so that I seemed to run now, the suitcase in my hand, as if I had not seen her in ten thousand years, had remembered her every second, and at last we were together forever, my desolation at long last relieved, and all the things in my life, all my possessions, my ambitions, my friends, my country, my world, like nothing, less than grains of sand before the beauty and joy of that exquisite and painful moment. I put my arms around her and began to cry. I slid down on my knees, happy with a vile and crushing happiness that nearly killed me with its terrible power. I could have spilled out my life then and there, so fierce was my joy for my woman.

"Now, now," one of the nurses said. "No more of that."

I got to my feet and kissed Joyce.

"He's my husband," she smiled. "Isn't he a darling?"

The nurses were not impressed. They fussed over her, tucked the blankets around her, and wheeled her inside.

The door closed before me. The room was number 1237. That was a good omen, for it contained my lucky number. I looked at my watch. It was 11:05. I went down the hall, passing many doors. Suddenly there was a hair-raising shriek. It came from a room up near the elevator, the cry of a woman in pain. A moment later I passed the room from whence the scream had come. Behind the door I heard a whimpering and crying, as if someone wept with her face buried in a pillow. It was a plaintive, pitiful lament, and it kept me worried, for I knew that this could happen to Joyce too.

There were two other fathers in the waiting room. They were exhausted men, their collars open, their ties hanging loosely. They looked like two men who had been in a bloodless, interminable barroom brawl. Sprawled out in leather chairs, their hair disheveled, cigarettes dangling from their hands, they paid no attention to me. I picked up a magazine and sat down. One of the fathers got to his feet and began pacing up and down. He smoked the tiniest of cigarettes, so small it burned his lips as he kissed rather than sucked it. Now the other father rose and began to pace too. Back and forth they paced, oblivious of one another, in a fury of caged walking, their foreheads wrinkled, each man trapped within the tensions of his own throbbing skull.

Around midnight, the taller of the two nurses who had attended Joyce appeared in the doorway. With the look of beaten dogs, the two fathers set their bloodshot eyes upon her. But it was me she wanted.

"You can see your wife now."

The two fathers looked at me with open mouths, watched me cross the room and go out the door. It was as if they had seen me for the first time, and were surprised that I had been in the room with them.

I followed the tall nurse.

"You mustn't stay long," she said. "Your wife needs rest."

Joyce lay in a hospital gown that tied up the back. Her hair had been combed in a tight high knot. There were handle bars at the head of her bed. She smiled, her face hot, fear jumping from her eyes. I took her hand.

"How do you feel?"

"Wonderful. I've had a shave and an enema."

"Are they good barbers?"

"They did a grand job. You're going to like it."

I was glad to find her out of the apologetic mood. But there was very little to say. We held hands, smiled foolishly, and looked at one another. The tall nurse opened the door.

"You'll have to leave now."

I kissed Joyce and stepped out into the hall.

"How long will it be?"

"A long time," the nurse said. "Why don't you go home and get some sleep?"

"I couldn't do that. It wouldn't be right."

"Don't be silly. The doctor won't be here until eight o'clock in the morning."

"You mean—she'll suffer that long?"

"She isn't suffering. And there's nothing you can do here. Absolutely nothing."

But a man cannot simply walk off and leave his pregnant wife alone in a room. It seemed an unheard-of, a crass and heartless thing. Even if the nurse was right, tradition insisted that I remain.

"I'll stay right here to the end," I said.

The nurse shrugged and made her eyebrows flutter.

"Once in a while we get a sensible father, but not often."

I went back to the waiting room.

The two self-mauled fathers had been joined by a fresh man. He was older, clean-shaven, neat in a brown suit. He gave off sweet vapors of comradeship and understanding. The haggard ones found him a sympathetic listener. Each took the floor to explain his troubles. The first man said his wife had been in labor thirteen hours. "Thirteen hours and forty-two minutes exactly," he said, looking at his watch. The older man clucked his tongue sadly. The other man put away his watch, sat down, grabbed his hair and resumed his agony. The second father wet his dry, cracked lips and his bleary eyes floated to the older man, who turned now, all kindness and wisdom, to hear his story. "My missus has been in there sixteen hours and twelve minutes," he said with a self-deprecating smile. This gave him a three-hour advantage over the first father, who hung his head in shame. But if the second father had a momentary taste of victory, it was quickly snatched away by the calm, older man.

"When Billy was born — he's our oldest boy — Mrs. Cameron was in labor fifty-three hours."

Mrs. Cameron's record time was so crushing that the two haggard fathers quickly lost interest in the kindly older man, who now turned his generous smile on me. But I had heard enough. These men were bragging, finding absurd consolations in their wives' anguish. The nurse was right. I decided to go home.

It was 1:30 when I got to bed. Out of Papa's room came the whistling snores. He didn't know Joyce was at the hospital. It seemed best not to waken him. I smoked a cigarette in the dark, and felt the fingers of guilt prodding me. Had I done the right thing? Maybe the tradition was sound. A man's wife lay in labor: should he not stay awake and contribute some small measure of self-inflicted pain as a symbol of his willingness to participate in their common heritage? After all, the tall nurse had nothing at stake here. She reasoned like a cold scientist. And in years to come, would it not fill our child with chagrin when he learned that

153

his own father had slept soundly as he made the perilous passage from the womb to life on the earth? I rolled and fretted, grappling with matters until three o'clock.

Then a fine and noble memory came back to me. I hopped out of bed and pulled my overnight bag out of the closet. In the side pocket I found it, a faded bouquet of sweet basil tied with red ribbon. I could not remember all of Mama's instructions. I could only recall something about hanging the bouquet from my bed. I fastened it to the crossbar of the headboard so that it fell to my pillow. Then I lay there, breathing its sweet and piquant aroma, and somehow it was the perfume of my mother's hair and her warm eyes smiled at me, and I began to cry because I didn't want to be a father, or a husband, or even a man, I wanted to be six or seven again, asleep in my mother's arms, and then I fell asleep, dreaming of my mother.

§ § §

Papa wakened me. It was seven o'clock.

"Somebody wants to talk."

I jumped out of bed and ran downstairs to the phone. It was the hospital. The nurse informed me that Joyce had not yet delivered the baby, but that she was doing fine.

"Is she in pain?"

"There's always some pain."

"I'm coming right down."

"I think you should."

Papa stood there, listening.

"The baby's coming, Papa. Any minute now."

The cigar trembled in his mouth.

"Where's Joyce?"

"The hospital. I took her there last night."

I rushed upstairs and dressed. When I went out to the car, there was Papa, waiting in the front seat. We drove to the hospital and took the elevator to the twelfth floor. A nurse ushered Papa into the waiting room. White-faced and frightened, he watched me hurry down the hall to Joyce's room.

She lay in a small ocean of pain, the vapors of her anguish clouding the room. She lay upon sheets wet and writhing with perspiration, her mouth distorted, her teeth clenched, her eyes like balls of white milk. At first she did not see me, but as I closed the door she lifted herself out of the waves of her suffering, her fingers clutching the iron bar across the top of the bed as she pulled herself into a sitting position. The white balloon was like an enormous blister, shimmering with pain, too heavy for the wild strength in her bloodless fingers. She panted in exhaustion, her breath coming in harsh jerks through lips twisted in torment.

Then she knew I was there at the foot of her bed. She saw me with startled eyes. My heart went out to her in pity for the blinding pain. I could not find words of consolation, only the clichés, the adumbrations and traps of futile language, the miserable inadequacies. As I stood there with a dry throat, pain seized her. Her knees came up and an animal cry, scarcely more than a suppressed howl, came from her lips. It had rhythm and could be measured, a thin coiling ribbon of noise drawn through her teeth. When it was over and the pain had spent itself, she sighed gratefully and pushed back a mass of wet disheveled hair, her eyes fixed at the ceiling. Then she remembered I was there.

"Oh, I'm such a coward!" she moaned.

"You're nothing of the kind."

I went to her side. The bed was built like a large crib, with adjustable steel sides. As I bent over to kiss her, I saw her red mouth, the lips thick with the sensuality of pain. I saw the white avid eyes and her suffering overwhelmed me. But there was passion in her mouth, and she clung to me with such ferocity that it took all the strength of my thick wrists to break her arms away. She loved me, she moaned, she loved me, loved me, loved me.

Then the pains took her again, sending her rolling from side to side, her knees up, her fingers pulling at the bar above her, the ribbon of anguish spilling out. As the suffering subsided, the white eyes beat about me like captured birds, and the pain reached me too, and I got a terrible stomach-ache. It nearly doubled me up. I backed into a chair and sat down. She was watching me.

"You're sick," she said. "This whole thing has been too much for you."

"I'm fine."

"Drink this," she panted, and she reached for a glass of water on the bed table. But the pains leaped at her as her hand went out, and she twisted and rolled, pouring out the ribbon of noise from her throat. It doubled me up in agony, but I didn't cry out, I just moaned as a crazy upheaval went on inside me, the pain of green apples.

"Darling," she was saying. "Call the doctor. I *know* you're sick!"

"Me? I feel wonderful."

But I could see my reflection in the wall mirror, and I was white and popeyed and disgusted and enraged with myself.

"Don't worry about me," she gasped. "I'm doing

wonderfully. The pains have stopped altogether. Look!" She held out her arms, smiling.

As I turned to see her, the pains were upon her again, and she struggled, her eyes softened now, full of tears, and when it was over again she covered her face with her hands and wept softly.

"Oh, God!" she cried. "I can't stand it much longer."

I would have done anything for her, my two arms, my feet, my hands, my life, all of it I would have given to lessen one pang of her anguish, but there I stood, unable to endure a spasmodic bellyache that finally sent me staggering, doubled up, into the hall.

Coming toward me was Dr. Stanley, and a nurse carrying a trayful of bottles and hypodermics.

They looked at me without speaking. Dr. Stanley took a phial of pills from the nurse's tray and tumbled one into his palm.

"Take this," he said.

I swallowed it in a fast gulp.

"My wife's in bad shape, Doc."

They sailed past me into the room. I waited. My bellyache subsided. In a few minutes they emerged, the doctor rubbing his hands.

"She's coming along beautifully."

"I tell you she's suffering terribly, Doc."

"Nonsense. She's had scopolamine. She won't remember a thing. We're taking her to the delivery room."

When they rolled her out of the room and down the hall, I hung back at first, pressed against the wall, afraid my presence would disturb her. But as she floated past I saw that she was asleep. They must have given her something, for her eyes were closed and her face was transformed into an image of white loveliness. I walked down the corridor at her side. Once she moaned. It was the murmur of one who had achieved ineffable peace after hours in the storm. It brought peace to me too. Now I knew that all was well, that the baby would soon be born, and Joyce would be all right.

I turned back to the waiting room. Papa sat in one of the big chairs, his arms folded, an iron silence holding him.

"Soon now," I said.

"What?" he whispered. "Nothing yet?"

"They've taken her to the delivery room."

"What's wrong with them?"

"They're doing all they can."

This made him growl, and I knew he felt I was conspiring with the hospital to keep the baby from being born. He stared ahead, saying no more.

A new crop of fathers sat in the waiting room, but their words were the same, the old wives' tales out of the mouths of baffled men. I couldn't stay there. Thinking of coffee, I left Papa in the waiting room and took the elevator to the hospital restaurant on the ground floor.

The place was full of nurses, doctors and internes. I sat at the counter and studied the menu. But I didn't want anything. In spite of everything, I was deeply worried. I walked out the side door to the street.

It was a dismal morning, the fog heavy and warm. I lit a cigarette and followed the sidewalk around the hospital grounds. The path was lined with tall eugenia hedges, immaculately clipped, a corridor of green that led to a garden where a fountain sprayed water among big red stones. I walked around the fountain, and the spray kissed my face with cool lips. Through the mist I saw the outline of a Gothic door. It was the hospital chapel. Suddenly, inexplicably, I began to cry, for here was the Thing I sought, the end of the desert, my house upon the earth. Eagerly I ran to the chapel.

Pax vobiscum! It was a small place, with only a crucifix at the main altar. I knelt as a tide of contrition engulfed me, a thundering cataract that roared in my ears. There was no need to pray, to beg forgiveness. My whole being lost itself in the deep drift, like waves returning to the shore. I was there for nearly an hour, and full of laughter as I rose to go. For it was a time for laughter, a time for great joy.

§ § §

Ten minutes later I saw the boy. He lay naked in the arms of a masked nurse. I couldn't touch him because they were behind a plate glass window. He was pinched and ugly like a gnome dipped in egg yolk. With a mustache, he would have looked just like his grandfather. He shrieked as the nurse exhibited him. I counted ten fingers, ten toes, and one penis. Certainly a father could ask for no more. I nodded and the nurse covered his dreadful little body with blankets and carried him somewhere into the complex machinery of the great hospital.

Then they wheeled Joyce out of the delivery room. She was very tired, smiling heavily.

"Did you see him?" she whispered.

I squeezed her hand.

"Don't talk now, darling. Sleep."

"It was wonderful," she sighed. "No pain, nothing."

She closed her eyes and they wheeled her down the hall.

§ § §

Papa was standing at the window in the waiting room. I put my hand on his shoulder and he turned. I didn't have to say anything. He began to cry. He laid his head on my shoulder and his weeping was very painful. I felt the bones of his shoulders, the old softening muscles, and I smelled the smell of my father, the sweat of my father, the origin of my life. I felt his hot tears and the loneliness of man and the sweetness of all men and the aching haunting beauty of the living.

I took him by the hand and we walked down the hall to the desk of the chief nurse. He covered his eyes with a red bandana into which his tears poured, and as he stood there crying, I told the nurse he wanted to see his grandson. He did not look at her, but his anguished joy was more than she could bear.

"It's against the rules," she said, "But . . ."

We followed her through swinging doors, Papa's hand in mine. She disappeared and a moment later she was on the other side of the glass, her face masked, holding the baby. Papa did not see the baby, for his two hands in the red handkerchief covered his eyes, but he knew the baby was very near, and he was struck with reverence, as if afraid to look upon the face of God. Even if he had raised his eyes, he would not have seen the baby for he was blind with tears. After a few moments the nurse took the baby away and I led Papa down the hall. He cried until we reached the car.

The ordeal had drained all his strength. He was in a kind of stupor as I drove home, his head against the car seat, his hands limp in his lap.

"I want to go home," he said.

"We'll be there in a few minutes."

"To San Juan. To Mama."

I looked at my watch. "The San Joaquin Daylight leaves in an hour. It's a fast train."

"I'll get my tools. You take me to the depot."

We drove on in silence. Gradually his strength returned. I parked the car in the street, before my house. We got out and he paused there to study the high peaked roof, the arched doorway.

"Good house," he said.

"Floor sags a little."

"Pooh. Don't mean nothing."

"We got a few termites."

"Everybody's got termites."

"But nobody's got a fireplace like mine."

He grinned and lit a cigar.

"It's a good one, kid. Plenty room for Santa Claus to come down the chimney."

"Papa, you know that piece of land near Joe Muto's place? You think I should buy it?"

"You stay right here and raise your family," he said.

We entered the house and I could hear him singing as he packed his things.

§ § §

Printed December 1987 in Santa Barbara & Ann Arbor
for Black Sparrow Press by Graham Mackintosh
& Edwards Brothers Inc. Design by Barbara Martin.
This edition is printed in paper wrappers; there
are 400 cloth trade copies; & 176 numbered deluxe
copies have been handbound in boards by Earle Gray.

JOHN FANTE was born in Colorado in 1909. He attended parochial school in Boulder, and Regis High School, a Jesuit boarding school. He also attended the University of Colorado and Long Beach City College.

Fante began writing in 1929 and published his first short story in *The American Mercury* in 1932. He had no difficulty in getting into print and published numerous short stories in *The Atlantic Monthly*, *The American Mercury*, *The Saturday Evening Post*, *Collier's*, *Esquire*, and *Harper's Bazaar*. His first novel, *Wait Until Spring, Bandini*, was published in 1938. The following year *Ask the Dust* appeared. (Both novels have been reprinted by Black Sparrow Press.) In 1940 a collection of his short stories, *Dago Red*, was published. *Full of Life* first appeared in 1952, and *The Brotherhood of the Grape* in 1977.

Meanwhile, Fante had been occupied extensively in screenwriting. Some of his credits include *Full of Life*, *Jeanne Eagles*, *My Man and I*, *The Reluctant Saint*, *Something for a Lonely Man*, *My Six Loves* and *Walk on the Wild Side*.

John Fante was stricken with diabetes in 1955 and its complications brought about blindness in 1978, but he continued to write by dictation to his wife, Joyce, and the result was *Dreams from Bunker Hill* (Black Sparrow, 1982). He died at the age of 74 on May 8, 1983.

In 1985 Black Sparrow published Fante's selected stories, *The Wine of Youth*, and two early novels, which had never before been published, *The Road to Los Angeles* and *1933 Was a Bad Year*. *West of Rome*, comprised of two previously unpublished novellas, was published by Black Sparrow in 1986.

DATE DUE

MAY 24	
	PRINTED IN U.S.A.